SUPER STORY TELLING

**Creative Ideas Using
Finger Plays, Flannel Board Stories,
Pocket Stories, and Puppets
With Young Children**

by
Carol Elaine Catron, Ed.D., The University of Tennessee
and
Barbara Catron Parks, M.S., Oak Ridge City Schools

Story illustrations by Jane Shasky,
based on original work of Martha Boone

Publishers
T. S. Denison & Company, Inc.
Minneapolis, Minnesota

 T. S. DENISON & COMPANY, INC.

Standard Book Number: 513-01793-3
Library of Congress Catalog Card Number: 85-52438
Copyright © 1986 by T. S. Denison & Co., Inc.
Minneapolis, Minnesota 55431-2590

CONTENTS

INTRODUCTION

Story telling is one very effective method for opening up the magic realm of fantasy, feelings, and fun with young children in a classroom setting. Children respond beautifully to a vital, creative, and involved story teller. Without great expense or abundant resources, you can provide a wide spectrum of props for story telling. Through story telling, children can experience:

- Mastery of listening skills.
- Extension of verbal language.
- Acquisition of sequencing skills.
- Discovery of feelings.
- Opportunities for role-play.
- Possibilities for self-direction.
- Fostering of creative expression.
- Growth of constructive socialization skills.
- Exercising control over the environment.
- Developing independence.

Super Story Telling contains finger plays, original stories, and classic folktales to use with young children. Reproducible flannel board, stick puppet and pocket story patterns are included. The book also has a section on using puppets in story telling, with suggestions and patterns for making many different kinds of puppets.

We recommend that you use a variety of techniques for story telling in your classroom:

- Verbal Story Telling: With our excitement over beautiful books and props, we sometimes neglect the age-old art of story telling, but it is basic, essential, and powerful. Know the story well; then use your voice, your mannerisms, and your body movements to convey emphasis and emotion. Although we have provided patterns for all the stories, we recommend interspersing stories told using visual props with stories told verbally without props.
- Finger Plays: These short rhyming stories are especially useful for filling in waiting times, transition times, and for introducing poetry to children.
- Flannel Board Stories: Teacher-made flannel board pieces are often creative and elaborate. Make your pieces durable so they can be handled by the children. Use our patterns, trace patterns from your favorite books, or make up your own.
- Puppets: Puppet masks, finger puppets, hand puppets, glove puppets, marionettes — the possibilities for creativity are endless!
- Dramatization: Utilize dramatic play props available in the classroom and let children role-play familiar stories or create their own new ones.
- Children's Books: Keep in mind the use of children's books in story telling. Know your age group and select appropriate books; some beautiful ones are available. Be particularly aware of sex role stereotyping and ethnic inequalities when making selections. Some of our favorites for reading, story telling, and dramatizing are included in the bibliography on pages 237-238. Don't forget the importance of child-dictated stories.

A resourceful teacher who genuinely enjoys children's stories, who is ready to listen and share and involve children in the story telling process, and who provides a classroom environment with creative props and cozy places for story telling, will help bring stories to life for young children. Story telling then becomes a way to learn about and appreciate the world, and sets the stage for a lifetime of adventures into the rich imaginary world of stories.

We encourage you to take our ideas and use them. Expand them by developing your own unique story telling style, creating your own stories, and involving your children in individual and group story telling activities. We invite you to enjoy the magic of story telling in your classroom!

FINGER PLAYS

Ten Dizzy Dragons

Ten dizzy dragons,
    Lived long, long ago,
In a land full of magic,
    Where few people could go.

The first dragon wore a garland of flowers;
The second dragon had strong magic powers.

The third dragon flew wildly through the air;
The fourth dragon lived in a jewel-filled lair.

The fifth dragon rescued people in trouble;
The sixth dragon like to blow pretty bubbles.

The seventh dragon wore a crown made of gold;
The eighth dragon had a heart brave and bold.

The ninth dragon had breath of smoky green fire;
The tenth dragon was a terrible, awful liar.

Ten dizzy dragons,
    Lived long, long ago,
In a land full of magic,
    Where in your dreams you can go.

Use the Ten Dizzy Dragons (see patterns on pages 10 to 14) on the flannel board. Make from pellon, using fabric paints for best results, or from felt.

#5

#6

#8

#7

#9

#10

Five Little Koala Bears

Five little koala bears in a eucalyptus tree,
The first one said, "Hey, look at me!"

The second one said, "I'm a pretty furry bear."
The third one said, "I don't have a care."

The fourth one said, "Australia is my home."
The fifth one said, "I'll never, ever roam!"

Five little koala bears in a eucalyptus tree,
Climbing and playing and happy to be free!

Use the Five Little Koala Bears (see patterns on pages 16 to 17) on the flannel board. Use pellon, felt, or fur for the bears.

koala bear—make 5

bottom of eucalyptus tree

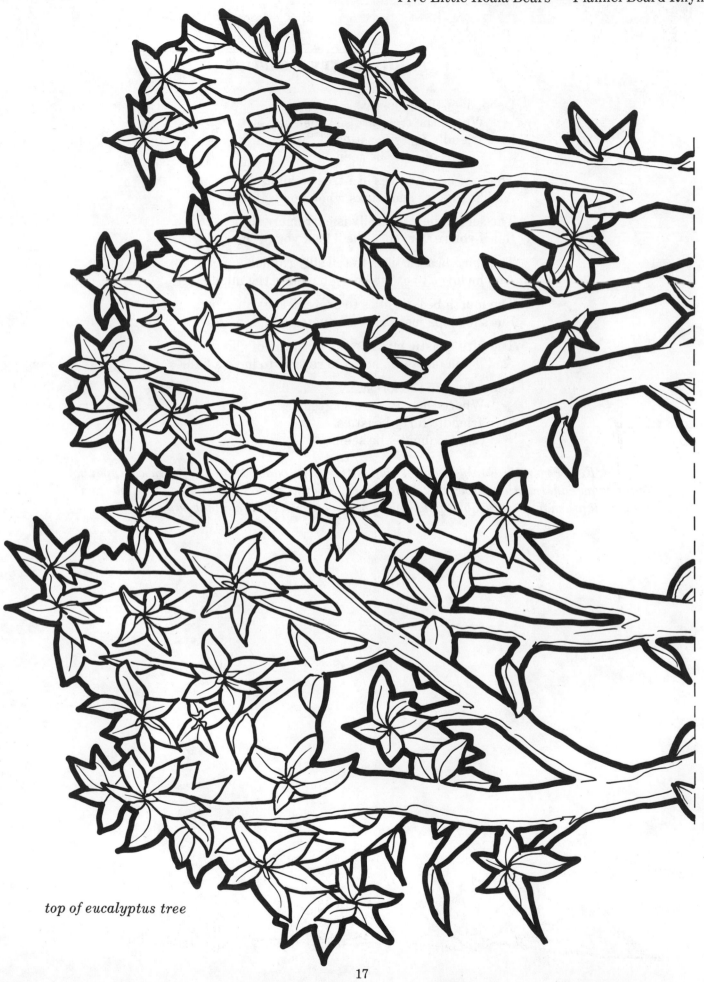

top of eucalyptus tree

Five Friendly Furry Beasties

Deep, deep in the forest,
    Where the trees are so green,
Five friendly furry beasties,
    Can frequently be seen.

The first beastie lives in a tree so high,
And he giggles and winks when you walk by.

The second beastie really is extremely shy,
But if you're very nice she'll look you in the eye.

The third beastie likes to tell silly riddles,
And he loves to eat so he's fat around the middle.

The fourth beastie likes to pretend she can growl,
But she stops just as soon as you give her a scowl.

The fifth beastie must be the most fun of all,
And if you play with her, you're sure to have a ball.

Deep, deep in the forest,
    Where the trees are so green,
Five friendly furry beasties,
    Can frequently be seen.

Use the Five Friendly Furry Beasties (see patterns on pages 19 to 20) as stick puppets. Make from construction paper or tag board, color with markers, and glue or staple to a tongue depressor. For durability, laminate or cover with clear contact paper.

#1

#2

Eight Giggling Ghosts

Eight giggling ghosts,
  Like to give you a fright,
When they come out to play,
  On a Halloween night.

One ghost laughs,
  And one ghost giggles;
One ghost ha-ha's,
  And one hoots and wiggles.

One ghost cackles,
  And one ghost roars;
One ghost guffaws,
  And one rolls on the floor.

Eight giggling ghosts,
  Aren't much of a fright,
When they come out to play,
  On a Halloween night.

Use the Eight Giggling Ghosts (see pattern on page 22) as stick puppets or flannel board characters.

giggling ghosts — make 8

Ten Little Christmas Elves

Ten little Christmas elves,
    Busy making lovely toys,
Helping Santa fill his list,
    For all good girls and boys.

The first elf painted a bright red truck;
The second elf added a quack to a duck.

The third elf dressed a pretty baby doll;
The fourth elf made a round orange ball.

The fifth elf stuffed a fuzzy teddy bear;
The sixth elf sewed a funny hat to wear.

The seventh elf put the wheels on a train;
The eighth elf wrapped up a candy cane.

The ninth elf drew pretty pictures in a book;
The tenth elf made gingerbread people to cook.

Ten little Christmas elves,
    Busy making lovely toys,
Helping Santa fill his list,
    For all good girls and boys.

Use the Ten Little Christmas Elves (see patterns on pages 24 to 28) as flannel board characters.

#1

#2

#3

#4

#5

#6

#8

#7

27

#9

#10

Ten Little Easter Bunnies

Ten little Easter bunnies with colored eggs so fine,
One hopped away and then there were nine.

Nine little Easter bunnies with ears so straight,
One hopped away and then there were eight.

Eight little Easter bunnies, as white as clouds in heaven,
One hopped away and then there were seven.

Seven little Easter bunnies with baskets made of sticks,
One hopped away and then there were six.

Six little Easter bunnies with smiles so alive,
One hopped away and then there were five.

Five little Easter bunnies with bonnets from the store,
One hopped away and then there were four.

Four little Easter bunnies feeling so free,
One hopped away and then there were three.

Three little Easter bunnies with coats like new,
One hopped away and then there were two.

Two little Easter bunnies playing in the sun,
One hopped away and then there was one.

One little Easter bunny, ready for some fun,
She hopped away and then there were none.

Use the Ten Little Easter Bunnies (see patterns on pages 30 to 32) as flannel board characters.

sun

#1, #2, #3 — make 3

#4

#6

#5

#10

#8, #9—make 2

#7

Six Marvelous Musicians

Six marvelous musicians,
     Dancing down the street,
Swaying to the rhythm,
     Playing music so sweet.

The first musician said,
     "My violin sounds grand."
The second musician said,
     "My flute's the best in the band."

The third musician said,
     "My bells sweetly chime."
The fourth musician said,
     "My tambourine keeps time."

The fifth musician said,
     "My drum goes rat-a-tat-tat."
The sixth musician said,
     "Oops! My horn sounds flat!"

Six marvelous musicians,
     Dancing down the street,
Swaying to the rhythm,
     Playing music so sweet.

Use the Six Marvelous Musicians (see patterns on pages 34 to 35) as stick puppets or flannel board characters.

"Six Marvelous Musicians" – Flannel Board Rhyme or Stick Puppets

#4

#5

#6

Ten Little Gingerbread Men

Ten little gingerbread men,
Baking brown in the oven;
One hopped up and out the door,
Ran down the lane and was seen no more.

Nine little gingerbread men,
Baking brown in the oven;
One hopped up and out the door,
Ran down the lane and was seen no more.

Eight little gingerbread men,
Baking brown in the oven;
One hopped up and out the door,
Ran down the lane and was seen no more.

Seven little gingerbread men,
Baking brown in the oven;
One hopped up and out the door,
Ran down the lane and was seen no more.

Six little gingerbread men,
Baking brown in the oven;
One hopped up and out the door,
Ran down the lane and was seen no more.

Five little gingerbread men,
Baking brown in the oven;
One hopped up and out the door,
Ran down the lane and was seen no more.

Four little gingerbread men,
Baking brown in the oven;
One hopped up and out the door,
Ran down the lane and was seen no more.

Three little gingerbread men,
Baking brown in the oven;
One hopped up and out the door,
Ran down the lane and was seen no more.

Two little gingerbread men,
Baking brown in the oven;
One hopped up and out the door,
Ran down the lane and was seen no more.

One little gingerbread man,
Baking brown in the oven;
He hopped up and out the door,
Ran down the lane and was seen no more.

The little old woman peeked inside,
And cried out "Eek!" for, to her surprise,
There were no little gingerbread men,
Baking brown in the oven.

Use the Ten Gingerbread Men (see pattern on page 38) as stick puppets. You could also purchase commercially available stickers and attach to tongue depressors.

gingerbread man—make 10

Six Busy Bears

Six little honey bears,
Going out to play.
Busy as can be,
On a fine spring day.

The first little bear's
Eating honey in a chair;
The second little bear's
Flying ballons in the air.

The third little bear's
Looking for rain in the sky;
The fourth little bear's
Riding her tricycle on by.

The fifth little bear's
Going fishing in the creek;
The sixth little bear's
Playing cowboy hide 'n seek.

Six little busy bears,
Tired as can be,
Hear Mama Bear calling,
"Come on home to me!"

Six little tired bears,
Better run home quick,
And away they all go—
One, two, three, four, five, six.   *(take bears off flannel board 1 by 1)*

Six little honey bears,
Will come out to play,
After a good night's sleep,
Another fine spring day.

Use patterns (see pages 40 to 46) to make flannel board characters.

bear eating honey

40

bear flying balloons

41

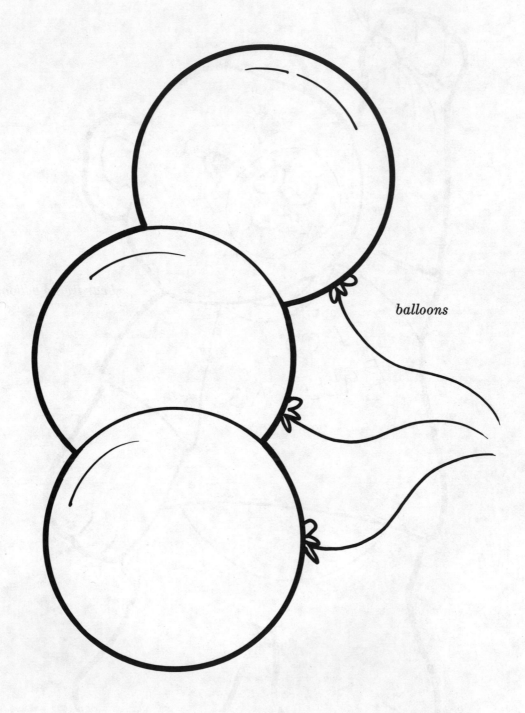

balloons

bear looking for rain

bear riding tricycle

bear going fishing

cowboy bear playing hide 'n seek

Eight Little Traveling Bears

Eight little traveling bears, sitting snug at home;
Dreamed of faraway places and decided to roam.
So they hugged and they kissed and they waved goodbye,
And one little traveling bear flew up toward the sky.

Seven little traveling bears, sitting snug at home;
Dreamed of faraway places and decided to roam.
So they hugged and they kissed and they hurried to the door,
And one little traveling bear bounced off to see more.

Six little traveling bears, sitting snug at home;
Dreamed of faraway places and decided to roam.
So they hugged and they kissed and they said, "See you soon!"
And one little traveling bear rode a rocket to the moon.

Five little traveling bears, sitting snug at home;
Dreamed of faraway places and decided to roam.
So they hugged and they kissed and they said farewell,
And one little traveling bear galloped off with a yell.

Four little traveling bears, sitting snug at home;
Dreamed of faraway places and decided to roam.
So they hugged and they kissed and they said, "We'll write!"
And one little traveling bear rode away on his bike.

Three little traveling bears, sitting snug at home;
Dreamed of faraway places and decided to roam.
So they hugged and they kissed and their bags were packed,
And one little traveling bear rode a train down the track.

Two little traveling bears, sitting snug at home;
Dreamed of faraway places and decided to roam.
So they hugged and they kissed and they held each other tight,
And one little traveling bear skated out of sight.

One little traveling bear, sitting snug at home;
Dreamed of faraway places and decided to roam.
She had hugged and she'd kissed and she just couldn't stay,
And one little traveling bear drove her truck away.

No little traveling bears, sitting snug at home;
Dreaming of faraway places—they all decided to roam.

Use patterns (see pages 48 to 50) as flannel board characters or stick puppets. Make from felt, fur, or tagboard.

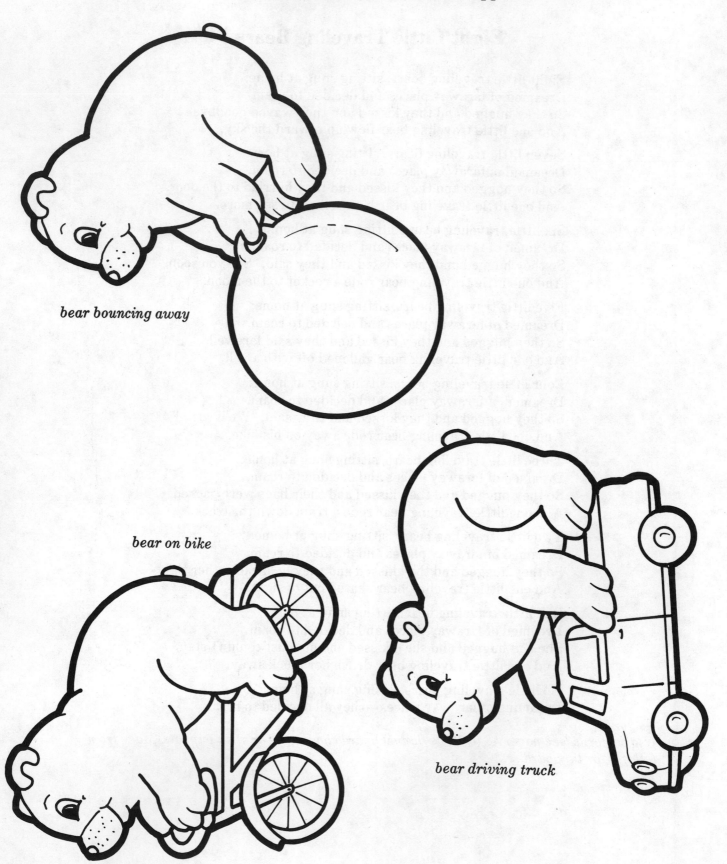

bear bouncing away

bear on bike

bear driving truck

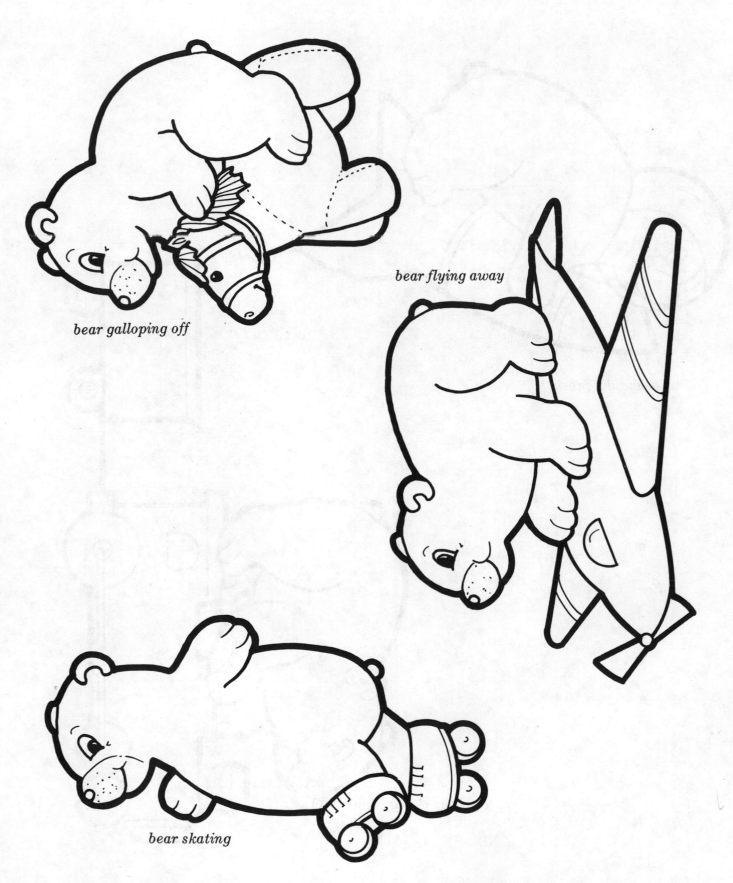

bear galloping off

bear flying away

bear skating

49

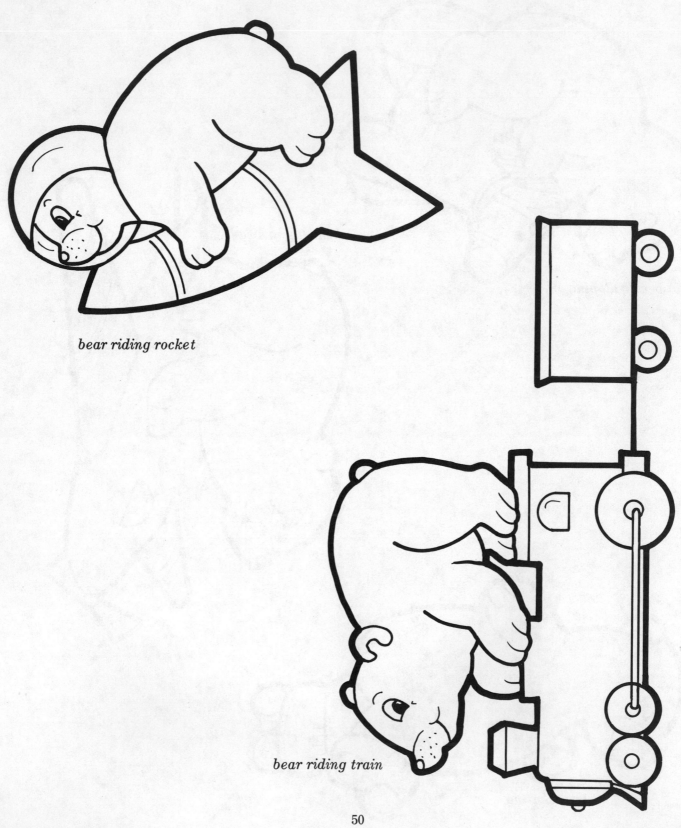

bear riding rocket

bear riding train

TRADITIONAL STORIES

We have included flannel board patterns for the traditional stories in this section. The traditional folk stories also lend themselves beautifully to dramatization because of their familiarity and the repetition involved in the stories. We have included some of our favorite ideas for dramatization below:

- **The Three Little Pigs** — Wooden climber-houses (that many early childhood education programs have as standard equipment) make excellent houses for the three pigs. Make masks for the little pigs and the wolf from paper bags or paper plates.

- **The Three Billy Goats Gruff** — Turn your rocking boat over for an instant bridge. Make character masks if desired, or just let the children assume the roles. This is a definite favorite!

- **Little Red Riding Hood** — Use dress-up clothes and housekeeping center props for acting out this story. Children could carry dolls as characters or make masks to fit the part.

- **The Three Bears** — Use a doll and three stuffed teddy bears as character props to tell this story. Use cots from the classroom as beds, and chairs and housekeeping center props to supply the additional items necessary to act out this special favorite.

- **The Gingerbread Boy** — This story is perfect as a vehicle for exploring a new environment at the beginning of the school year. Tell the story several times, until the children are very familiar with it. Then have a cooking activity with your children, baking one large gingerbread man. After the gingerbread man is done baking, have him run away (arrange this disappearance with another teacher). The gingerbread man can leave a trail of notes behind him, saying, "Run, run, as fast as you can. You can't catch me. I'm the gingerbread man! Now I'm running to the motor lab!," etc. The children will find another note in each new place they follow the gingerbread man to. Enlist the help of other teachers, principals or directors, cooks, etc., to take the children to the various places in your school or center. Finally, they should find a note sending them back to their own classroom, where the gingerbread man will be waiting to be eaten up as a delicious snack!

The Three Little Pigs

Once upon a time, there was a mother pig who had three little pigs. As the little pigs grew up, the mother pig sent the young ones out into the world to make their fortunes.

One fine morning, the three little pigs started out into the wide world, each along a different road.

The first little pig walked along in the wide world until he met a man with a load of straw. "Please, Mr. Man," said the pig, "give me some straw so I can build a little house." The man gave the first little pig some straw, and he built himself a house.

The second little pig walked along in the wide world until he met a man with a load of sticks. "Please, Mr. Man," said the pig, "give me some sticks so I can build a little house." The man gave the second little pig some sticks, and he built himself a house.

The third little pig walked along in the wide world until he met a man with some bricks. "Please, Mr. Man," said the pig, "give me some bricks so I can build a little house." The man gave the third little pig some bricks, and he built himself a house.

The first little pig had just moved into his straw house when a big, bad wolf came along. "Little pig, little pig, let me come in!" the wolf called.

"Not by the hair of my chinny, chin, chin," answered the first little pig.

"If you don't," said the wolf, "I'll huff and I'll puff and I'll blow your house in!"

But the first little pig wouldn't let the big, bad wolf in. So the wolf huffed and he puffed and he blew the house in! The first little pig ran away to his brother's house just as the straw house was falling down.

The second little pig had just moved into his stick house when his first brother ran in, with the big, bad wolf close behind him. "Little pigs, little pigs, let me come in!" the wolf called.

"Not by the hair of our chinny, chin, chins," answered the two little pigs.

"If you don't," said the wolf, "I'll huff and I'll puff and I'll blow your house in!"

But the two little pigs wouldn't let the big, bad wolf in. So the wolf huffed and he puffed and he blew the house in! The two little pigs ran away to their third brother's house just as the stick house was falling down.

The third little pig had just moved into his house of bricks when his two little brothers ran in, with the big, bad wolf close behind them. "Little pigs, little pigs, let me come in!" the wolf called.

"Not by the hair of our chinny, chin, chins," answered the three little pigs.

"If you don't," said the wolf, "I'll huff and I'll puff and I'll blow your house in!"

But the three little pigs wouldn't let the big, bad wolf in. So the wolf huffed and he puffed, and he puffed and he huffed, but he couldn't blow the house in. So the clever wolf climbed up on the roof of the little brick house, and he called down the chimney, "Now, little pigs, I am coming down to eat you up!"

"Oh, are you?" called the little pigs, and they took the lid off a huge pot of water bubbling on the fire, just as the wolf jumped down the chimney. Down came the wolf, and he landed in the pot of boiling water. The wolf howled in pain and went back up the chimney as fast as he could. That was the end of the big, bad wolf — he ran away forever. And the three little pigs lived happily ever after in the little brick house.

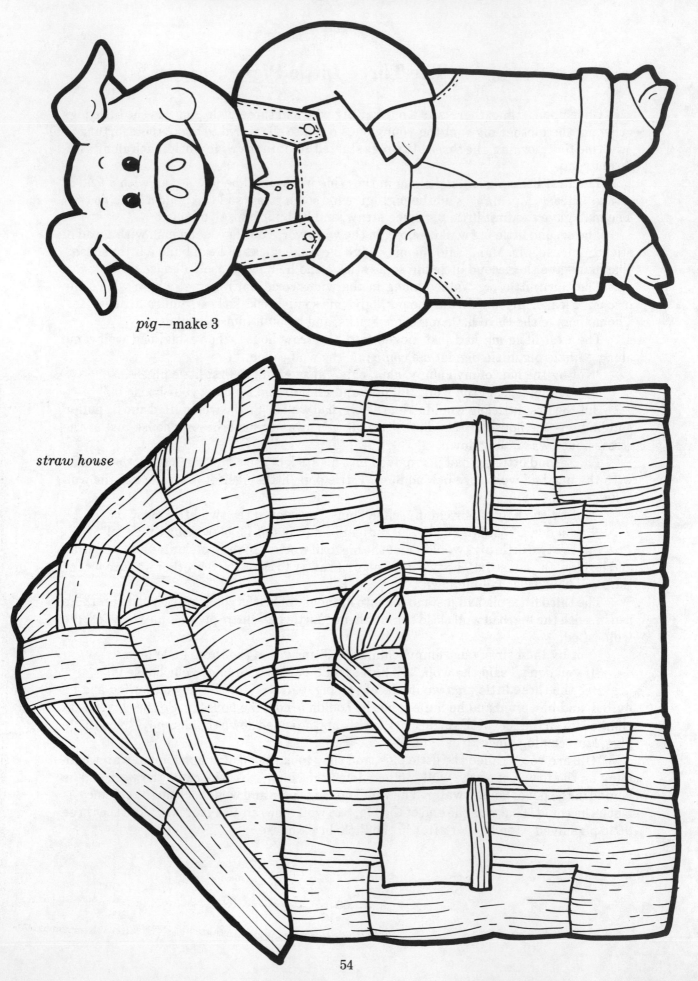

pig—make 3

straw house

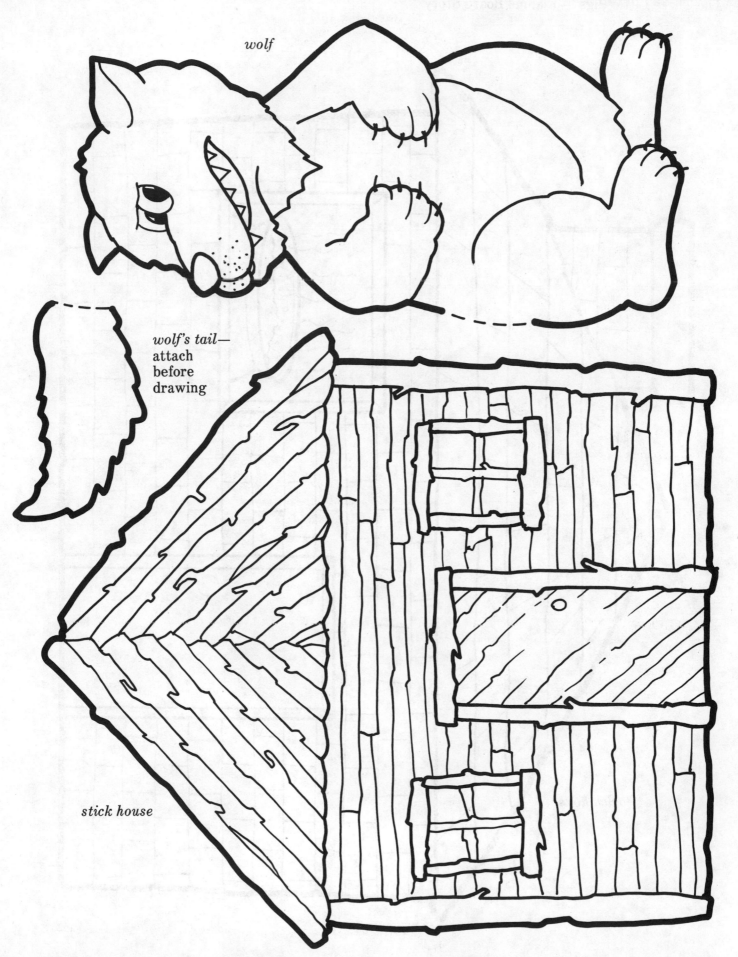

wolf

wolf's tail—
attach
before
drawing

stick house

55

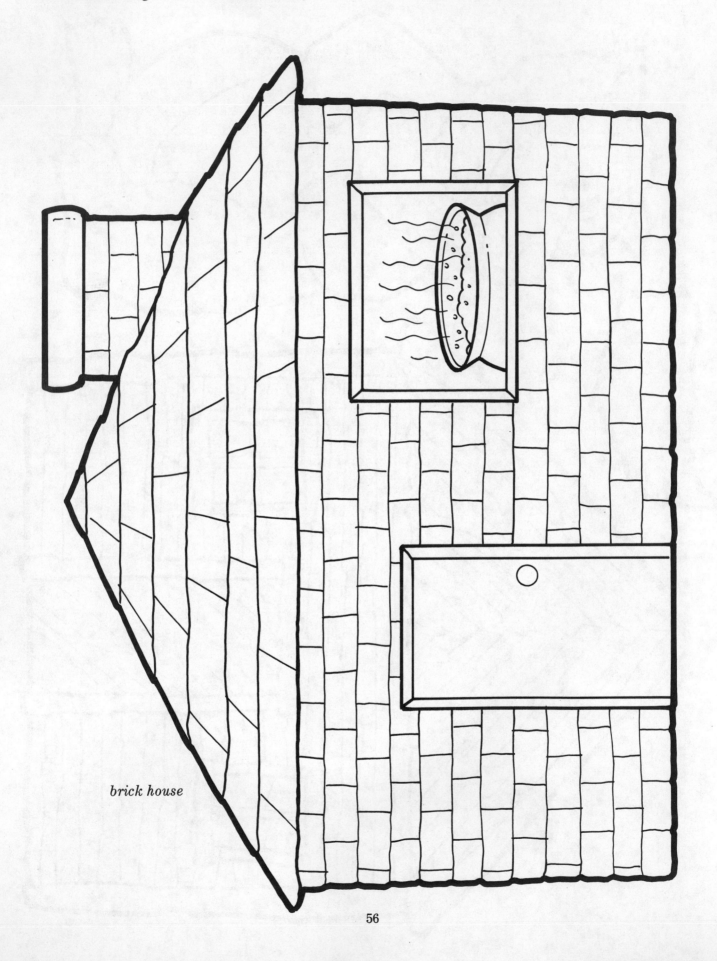

brick house

The Three Billy Goats Gruff

Once upon a time, a long, long time ago, when the world was very young, there lived three billy goats named Gruff. There was a Big Billy Goat Gruff, a Middle-Sized Billy Goat Gruff, and a Little Billy Goat Gruff. The Three Billy Goats Gruff lived together on a mountainside. Now on their mountainside they had eaten most of the grass, but just across the way was a beautiful pasture of green grass. On the way to this pasture they had to pass over a bridge, and under the bridge lived a big, ugly troll.

One day the Three Billy Goats Gruff decided to cross the bridge to get to the beautiful pasture of green grass on the other side. First the Little Billy Goat Gruff started across the bridge, trip-trap, trip-trap.

"Who's that tripping across my bridge?" roared the troll.

"It's only I, the Little Billy Goat Gruff," answered the Little Billy Goat softly.

"I'm coming up to eat you," shouted the troll.

"Oh, please, Mr. Troll, don't eat me," said the Little Billy Goat. "Why don't you wait for my bigger brother who will be coming this way soon?"

The troll grumbled and rumbled, but he let the Little Billy Goat Gruff cross the bridge.

Soon the Middle-Sized Billy Goat Gruff came trip-trap, trip-trap across the bridge.

"Who's that tripping across my bridge?" roared the troll.

"It's only I, the Middle-Sized Billy Goat Gruff," answered the Middle-Sized Billy Goat.

"I'm coming up to eat you," shouted the troll.

"That would be very foolish, indeed," said the Middle-Sized Billy Goat Gruff. "Wait for my bigger brother who will be coming this way very soon."

The troll grumbled and rumbled, but he let the Middle-Sized Billy Goat Gruff cross the bridge.

After a while the Big Billy Goat Gruff came trip-trap, trip-trap across the bridge.

"Who's that tripping across my bridge?" roared the troll.

"It is I, the Big Billy Goat Gruff," answered the Big Billy Goat.

"I'm coming up to eat you," shouted the troll.

"Come ahead!" the Big Billy Goat Gruff shouted back.

When the big, ugly troll came up, the Big Billy Goat Gruff lowered his big, strong head and butted the troll off the bridge right into the river. The troll was never seen again.

Then the Big Billy Goat Gruff joined his brothers in the green pasture. The grass was delicious and the Three Billy Goats Gruff grew fat and content and lived happily together ever after.

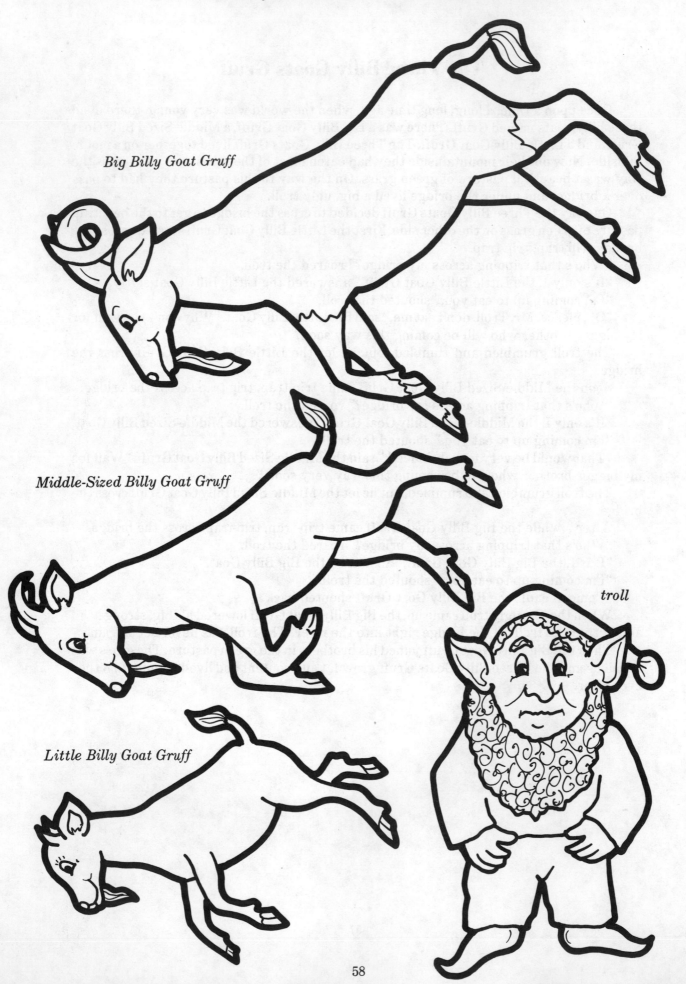

Big Billy Goat Gruff

Middle-Sized Billy Goat Gruff

Little Billy Goat Gruff

troll

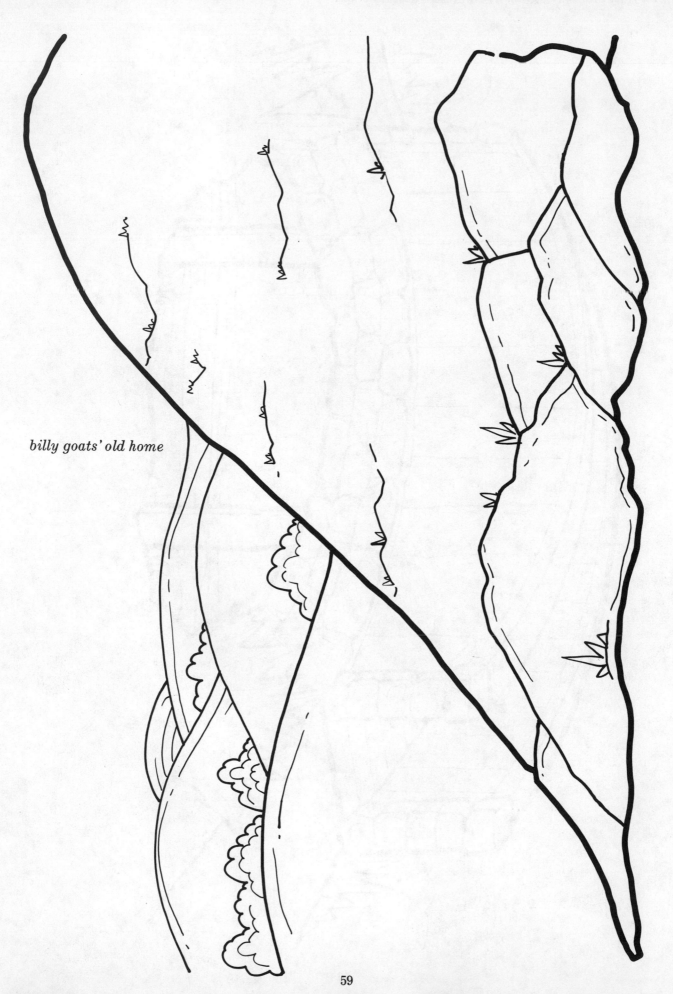

billy goats' old home

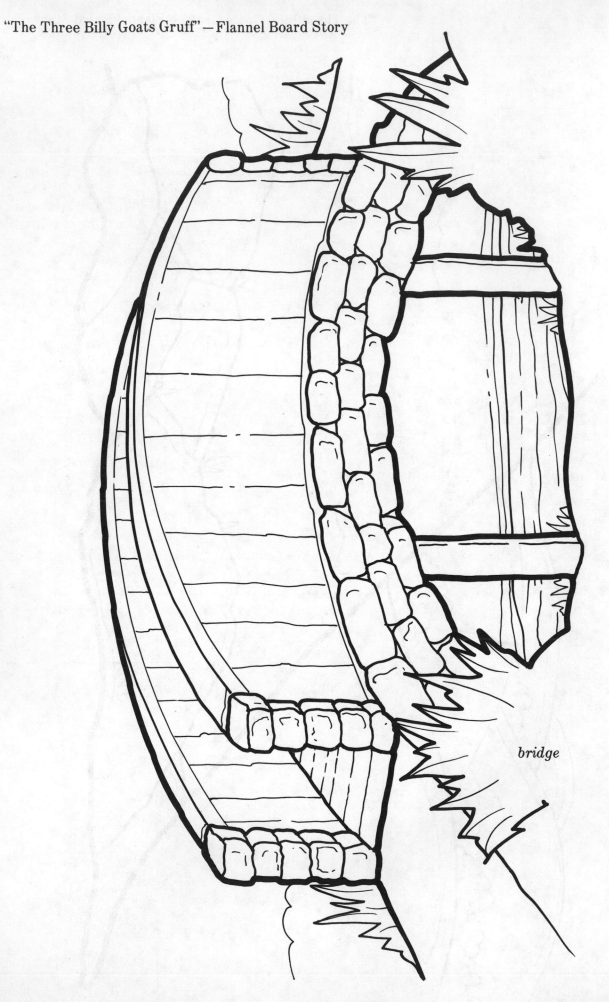

bridge

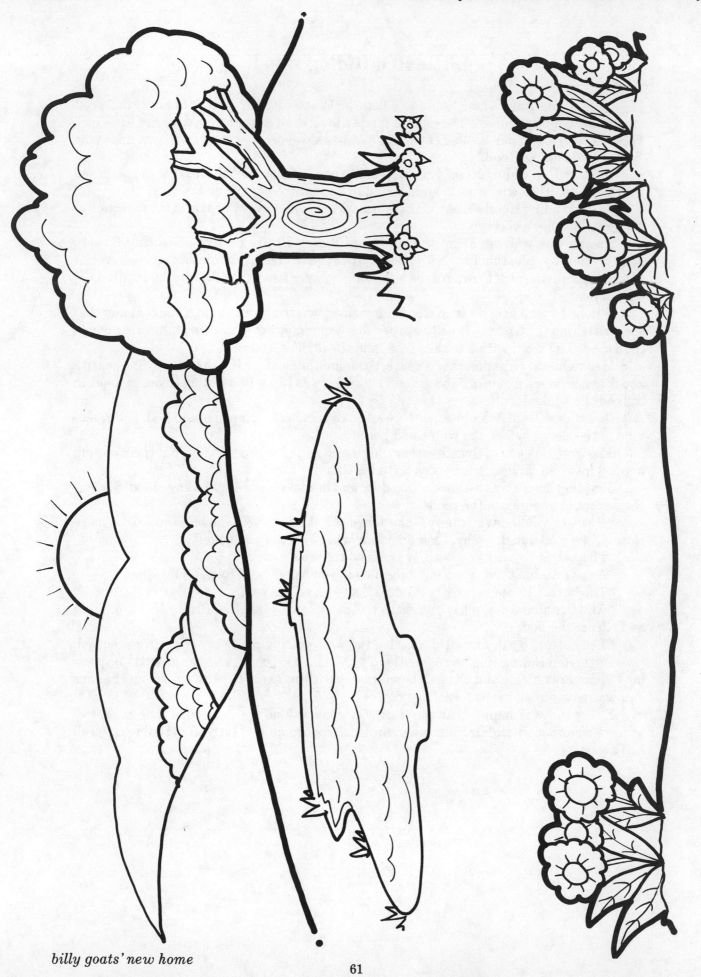

billy goats' new home

Little Red Riding Hood

Once upon a time, a long time ago, a little girl lived with her mother in a cozy little cottage at the edge of a forest. The mother made a lovely red cape and hood for her little girl. The little girl loved her hooded cape, and because she wore it so much, she was known as "Little Red Riding Hood."

One day Red Riding Hood's mother said to her, "Please take this basket of goodies to your Grandmother who is sick, and don't stop and talk to anyone on the way."

So Red Riding Hood set out with the basket of goodies over her arm in the direction of her grandmother's cottage.

As she was walking along the path, Red Riding Hood saw some beautiful flowers growing nearby. She thought, "How nice it would be to take Grandmother some flowers," and she stopped to pick them. As she was stooping over to pick the flowers, suddenly a big wolf appeared!

When the wolf asked Little Red Riding Hood where she was going, she told him that she was taking the basket of goodies to her sick Grandmother, who lived at the other end of the forest. The wolf, with a wicked plan in his head, hurried away.

Meanwhile at Grandmother's house, Grandmother was tucked in her bed. She heard a knock at her door. "Come in," she called, thinking it was Little Red Riding Hood. Instead, in walked the wicked wolf.

Quick as a flash, Grandmother threw the covers back, jumped out of bed, and ran to hide in the closet before the wolf could get her.

The wolf took one of Grandmother's nightgowns and one of her caps, put them on, and hopped into bed, pulling the covers up to his chin.

Just then there was a knock at the door and in came Little Red Riding Hood. She put the basket of goodies on the table.

"How are you today, Granny?" she asked. As she bent over the bed and looked more closely, she exclaimed, "Why, Grandmother, what big ears you have!"

"The better to hear you with," answered the wolf.

"And Grandmother, what big, bright eyes you have!" said Red Riding Hood.

"The better to see you with, my dear," answered the wolf.

"And Grandmother, what big, sharp teeth you have!" said Red Riding Hood, backing away from the bed.

"The better to eat you with!" snarled the wolf, getting ready to spring from the bed.

Little Red Riding Hood screamed loudly. A kind woodsman, who happened to be passing by, came in quickly and chased the wolf away with his axe. The big wolf ran out the door and was never seen in the forest again.

Everyone was happy that the wolf was gone and no one was hurt. The basket of goodies was opened, and Grandmother, the kind woodsman, and Little Red Riding Hood all had a party.

"Little Red Riding Hood"—Flannel Board Story

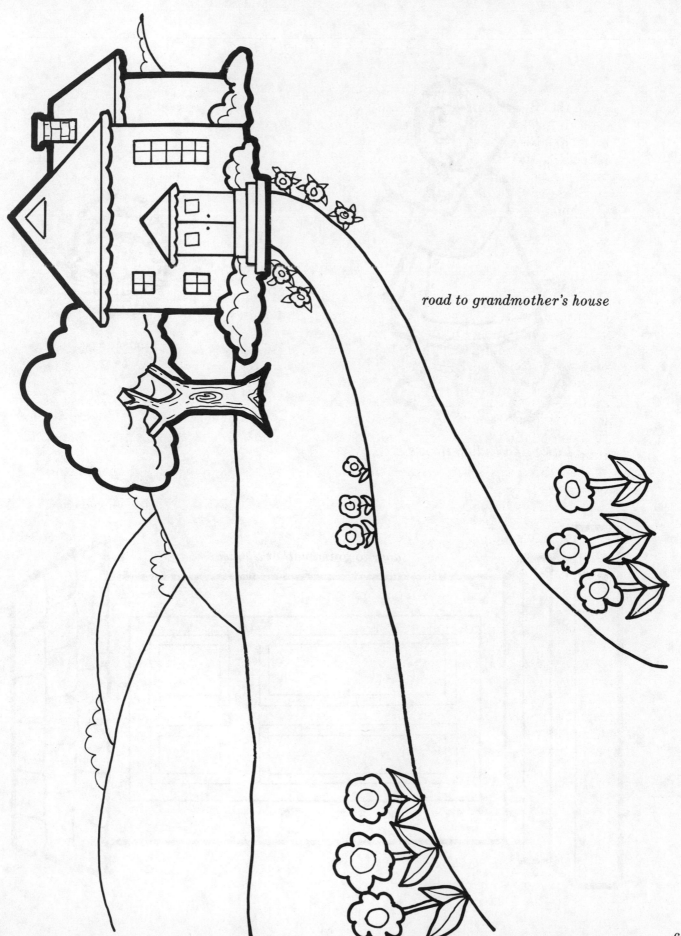

road to grandmother's house

Little Red Riding Hood

basket

door to grandmother's house

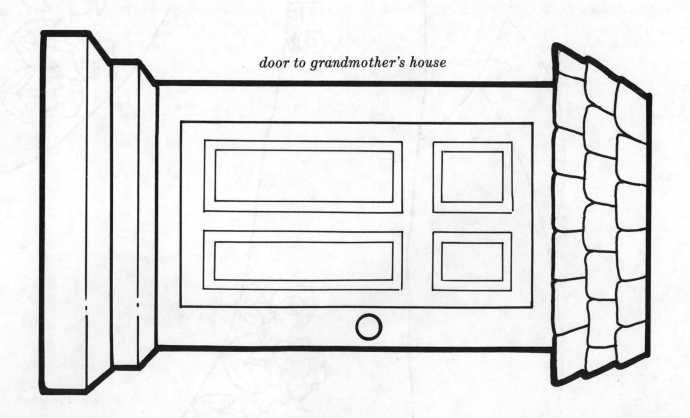

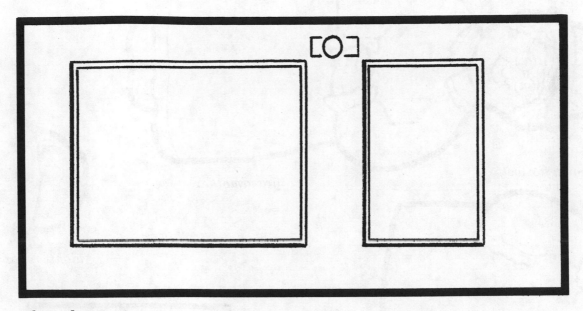

closet door

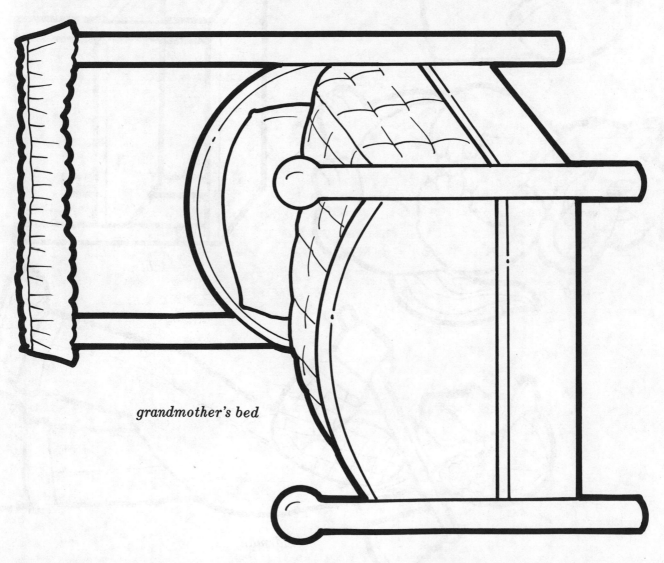

grandmother's bed

nightgown for wolf

grandmother

nightcap for wolf

wolf

table

woodsman

The Three Bears

Once upon a time Three Bears lived in a little cottage in the woods. One was a great big Papa Bear. One was a middle-sized Mama Bear. And one was a wee little Baby Bear.

They each had a bowl for their porridge. Papa Bear had a great big bowl. Mama Bear had a middle-sized bowl. Baby Bear had a wee little bowl.

They each had a chair to sit in. Papa Bear had a great big chair. Mama Bear had a middle-sized chair. Baby Bear had a wee little chair.

And they each had a bed to sleep in. Papa Bear had a great big bed. Mama Bear had a middle-sized bed. Baby Bear had a wee little bed.

One morning Mama Bear prepared a good breakfast of hot porridge for her family. When the porridge was cooked, Mama Bear put some in Papa Bear's great big bowl, some in her own middle-sized bowl, and some in Baby Bear's wee little bowl. Then she called her family to breakfast.

Papa Bear took a great big gulp, and declared in a great big voice, "My porridge is too hot!" Mama Bear tasted her porridge and in her middle-sized voice said, "My porridge is too hot, too!" Then the Baby Bear in his wee little voice squeaked, "My porridge is too hot, too!" Papa Bear said, "Why don't we take a walk in the woods while the porridge cools?"

While the Three Bears were taking their walk, a pretty little girl with golden curls, called Goldilocks, came up to the cottage in the woods. First she peeked in the window. Next she knocked at the door, but no one answered. Then she smelled the porridge! "Hi!" she called. "Is anyone home?" There was no answer, so Goldilocks pushed open the door, walked in, and looked around.

She saw the three bowls of porridge cooling on the table. "It smells good," she said. "I'm so hungry. I think I'll taste just a little." First Goldilocks tasted the porridge from Papa Bear's great big bowl. "This is too hot!" she said. She tasted the porridge in Mama Bear's middle-sized bowl. "This is too cold!" she said, shaking her head. Then she tasted the porridge in Baby Bear's wee little bowl and said, "This is just right!" It was so yummy that Goldilocks ate it all up!

Full from the porridge, Goldilocks wandered into the living room and decided to try out the three chairs. First she tried the great big chair belonging to Papa Bear. "This one is too hard!" said Goldilocks. Next she tried the middle-sized chair belonging to Mama Bear. "This one is too soft!" she said. Then she tried Baby Bear's wee little chair. "This one is just the right size," said Goldilocks. But she sat down too hard, and . . . snap, crack, clatter . . . down went the little chair into little pieces.

Goldilocks was tired after the chair broke. She wandered upstairs and found three beds. She decided to take a nap on whichever bed was the most comfortable. First Goldilocks tried Papa Bear's great big bed. "This is much too hard!" said Goldilocks. Next she tried Mama Bear's middle-sized bed. Plop! Goldilocks sank down deep into the middle of the bed. "This one is much too soft!" she said. But Baby Bear's wee little bed felt so comfortable and cozy. Goldilocks yawned. "This bed is just right!" she said. And soon she was sound asleep.

Meanwhile, the Three Bears came home from their walk in the woods, ready to eat a good breakfast. Papa Bear went over to his great big bowl and found some of his porridge was gone. He said in his great big voice, "Someone has been eating my porridge." Mama Bear found some of her porridge gone, and said in her middle-sized voice, "Someone has been eating my porridge!" Then Baby Bear in his wee little voice squeaked, "Someone has been eating my porridge, and they ate it all up!"

Papa Bear thumped into the living room and said in his great big voice, "Someone has been sitting in my chair!" Then Mama Bear in her middle-sized voice exclaimed, "Someone has been sitting in my chair!" Then the Baby Bear in his wee little voice squeaked, "Someone has been sitting in my chair, and they broke it all to pieces!"

Up the stairs, on tiptoe, went the Three Bears. In his great big voice Papa Bear declared, "Someone has been sleeping in my bed!" In her middle-sized voice Mama Bear exclaimed, "Someone has been sleeping in my bed!" In his wee little voice Baby Bear squeaked, "Someone has been sleeping in my bed, and there she is!"

Goldilocks woke up with the sound of the Three Bear's voices. She took one frightened look at the bears, scampered out of bed, hurried down the stairs and out the door, and ran home as fast as her little legs could carry her!

When the excitement was all over, Papa Bear fixed Baby Bear's broken chair and Mama Bear cooked more porridge. And in the end the Three Bears settled down to eat their breakfast.

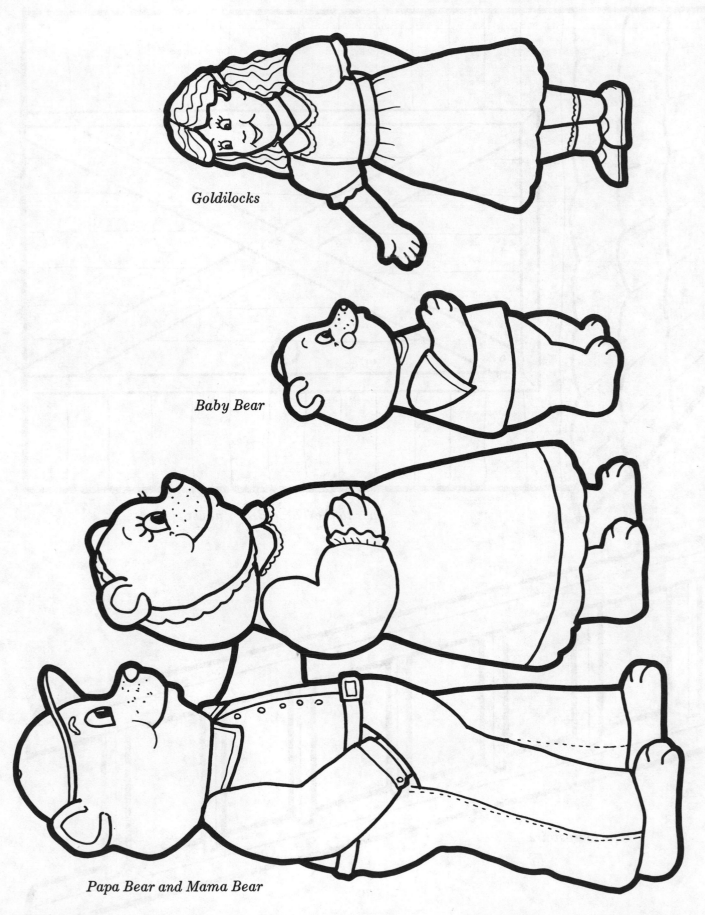

Goldilocks

Baby Bear

Papa Bear and Mama Bear

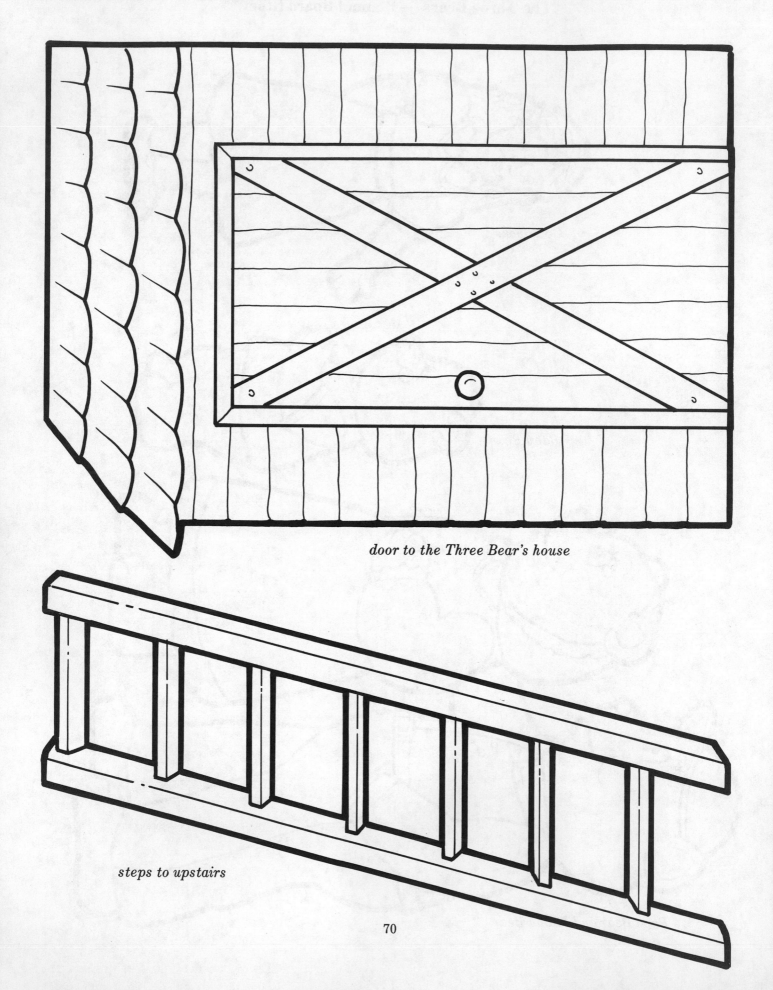

door to the Three Bear's house

steps to upstairs

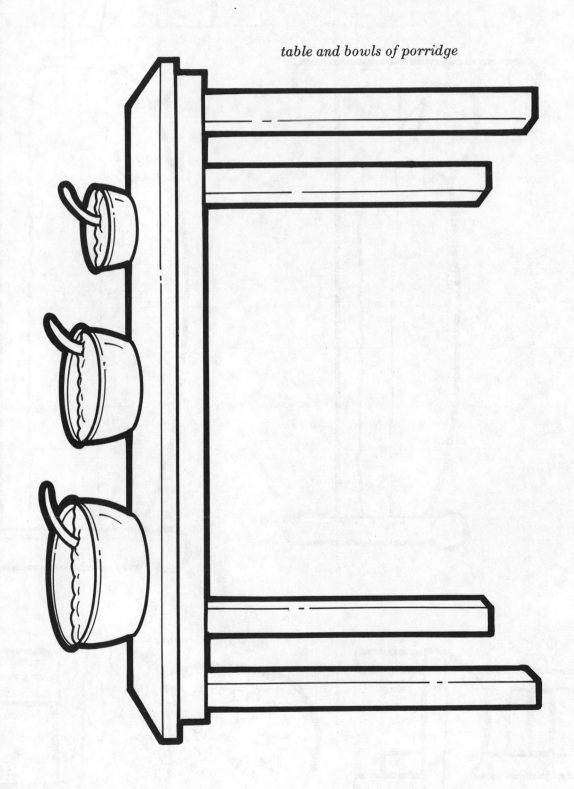

table and bowls of porridge

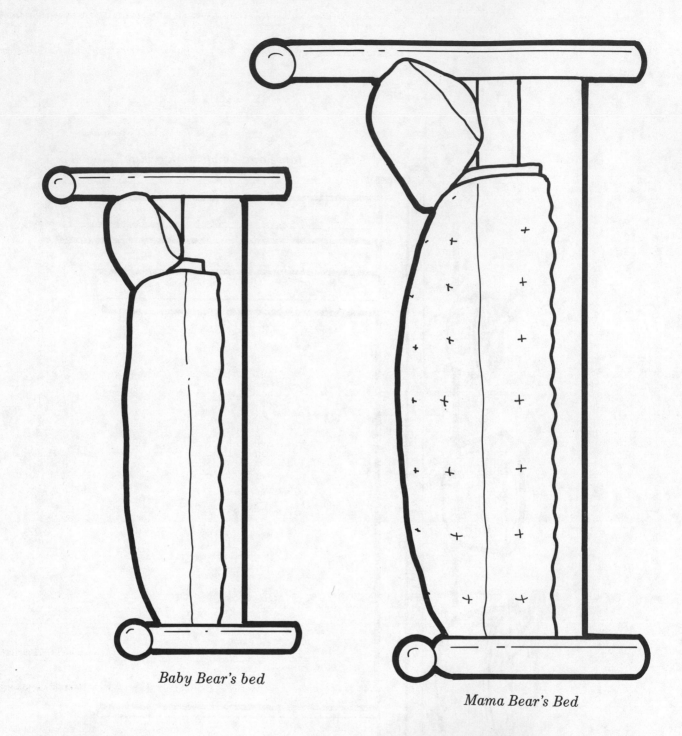

Baby Bear's bed

Mama Bear's Bed

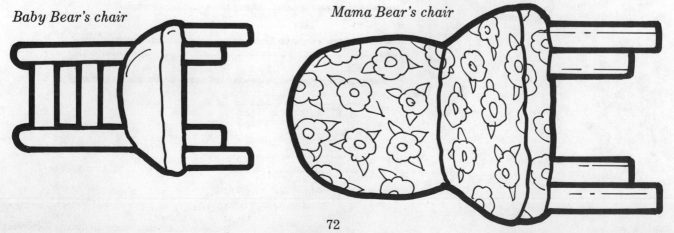

Baby Bear's chair

Mama Bear's chair

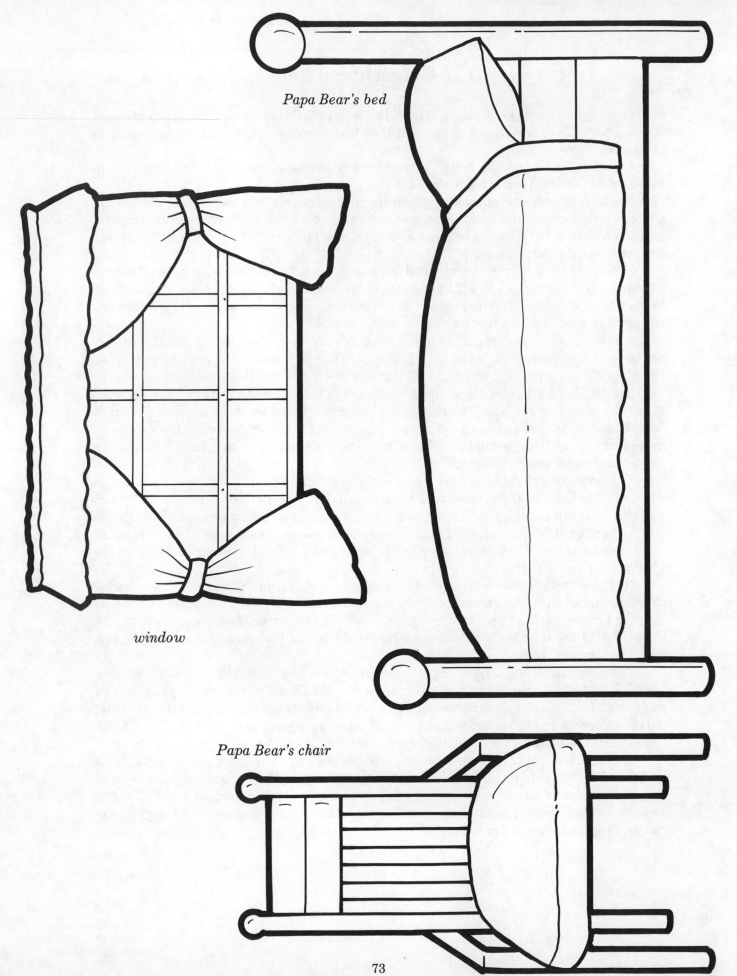

Papa Bear's bed

window

Papa Bear's chair

The Gingerbread Boy

Once upon a time there lived a little old man and a little old woman in a little old house in the woods. They were very happy, but they had no children and they did want a little child of their own.

One morning when the little old woman was baking gingerbread, she chuckled to herself and said, "I'll make my little old man a gingerbread boy."

So she took a piece of spicy dough, and she rolled it out smooth, and she cut it out in the shape of a fine gingerbread boy. She gave him raisins for eyes, and a wide smiling mouth, and down the front of his jacket she put a row of currant buttons. Then, with a little pat, she popped him into the hot oven.

When she thought the gingerbread boy should be baked clean through, the little old woman, still chuckling to herself, opened the oven door to peek in. But before she had time to put a finger on him, the gingerbread boy hopped right out of the oven, skipped through the kitchen door, and ran down the path to the woods.

The little old woman ran after him, calling, "Come back, come back!" But the gingerbread boy only laughed and cried out, "Run, run as fast as you can. You can't catch me. I'm the gingerbread man!" He was right. The little old woman could not catch him.

The little old man saw the gingerbread boy run past with the little old woman after him. "Come back, come back," he called. But the gingerbread boy only laughed and cried out, "Run, run as fast as you can. You can't catch me. I'm the gingerbread man! I've run away from the little old woman, and I can run away from you, too, I can, I can." Then away down the road he dashed.

The gingerbread boy ran past a cow eating grass in a field. The cow called, "Come back, come back!" But the gingerbread boy only laughed and cried out, "Run, run as fast as you can. You can't catch me. I'm the gingerbread man! I've run away from the little old woman and the little old man, and I can run away from you, too, I can, I can." The cow chased after the gingerbread boy, thinking he would make a nice lunch, but he could not catch the gingerbread boy either.

Next the gingerbread boy ran past some farmers in the field. "Come back, come back," they called. But the gingerbread boy only laughed and cried, "Run, run as fast as you can. You can't catch me. I'm the gingerbread man! I've run away from the little old woman, the little old man and the cow, and I can run away from you, too, I can, I can." And away he ran, with the farmers trailing behind him.

Then the gingerbread boy ran past a pig in his pen. The pig called, "Come back, come back!" But the gingerbread boy only laughed and cried, "Run, run as fast as you can. You can't catch me. I'm the gingerbread man! I've run away from the little old woman, the little old man, the cow and the farmers, and I can run away from you, too, I can, I can." And away the gingerbread boy ran, with all of them far behind him.

A fox peeked out of hiding as the gingerbread boy ran past, and his sharp eyes shone hungrily. "Watch out, gingerbread boy," he called. The gingerbread boy only laughed and cried, "Run, run as fast as you can. You can't catch me. I'm the gingerbread man! I've run away from the little old woman, the little old man, the cow, the farmers and the pig. I can run away from you, too, I can, I can."

But the fox did not run after him. He just said sweetly, "I don't want to catch you, gingerbread boy. But there is a river just ahead, and I will give you a ride across on my tail if you like, so that the little old woman, the little old man, the cow, the farmers and the pig will not be able to catch you."

The gingerbread boy looked at the river ahead. He looked behind him. Then he looked at the fox. "Kind fox, since your tail is so far from your mouth, I will accept the ride," he called. So he hopped onto the fox's tail and they started across the river. As the water grew deeper, the fox called to the gingerbread boy, "Hop on my back or you will get wet."

So the gingerbread boy hopped up onto the fox's back, and on they went. Then the water got still deeper and the fox called out, "Hop on my head or you will get wet." So the gingerbread boy hopped up on to the fox's head. Suddenly the sly fox flipped his head and opened his mouth and in popped the gingerbread boy.

And that was the end of the gingerbread boy!

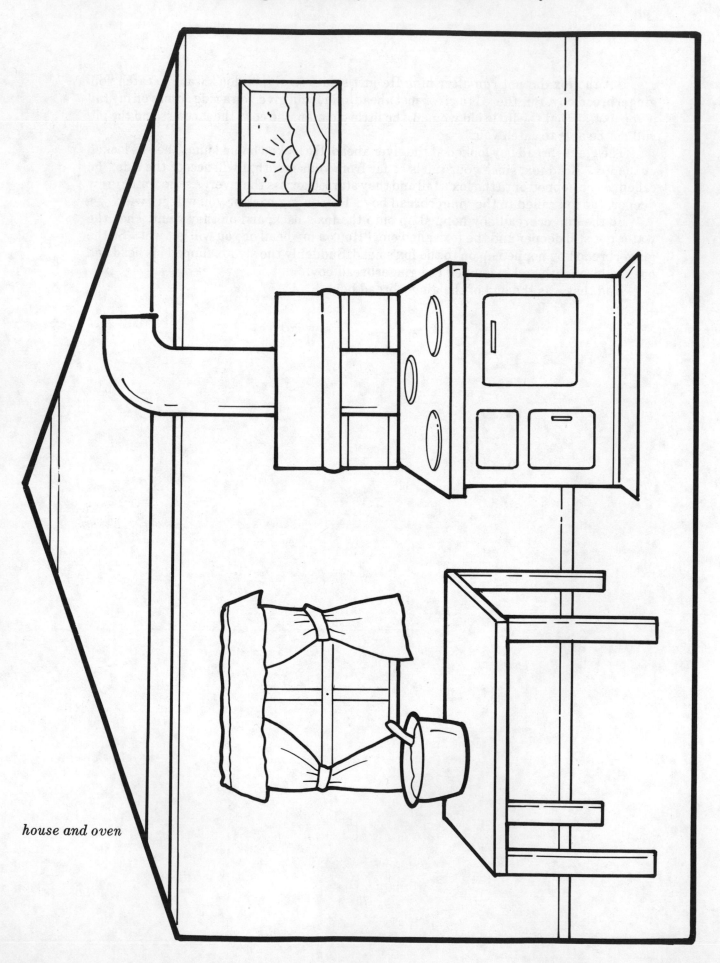

house and oven

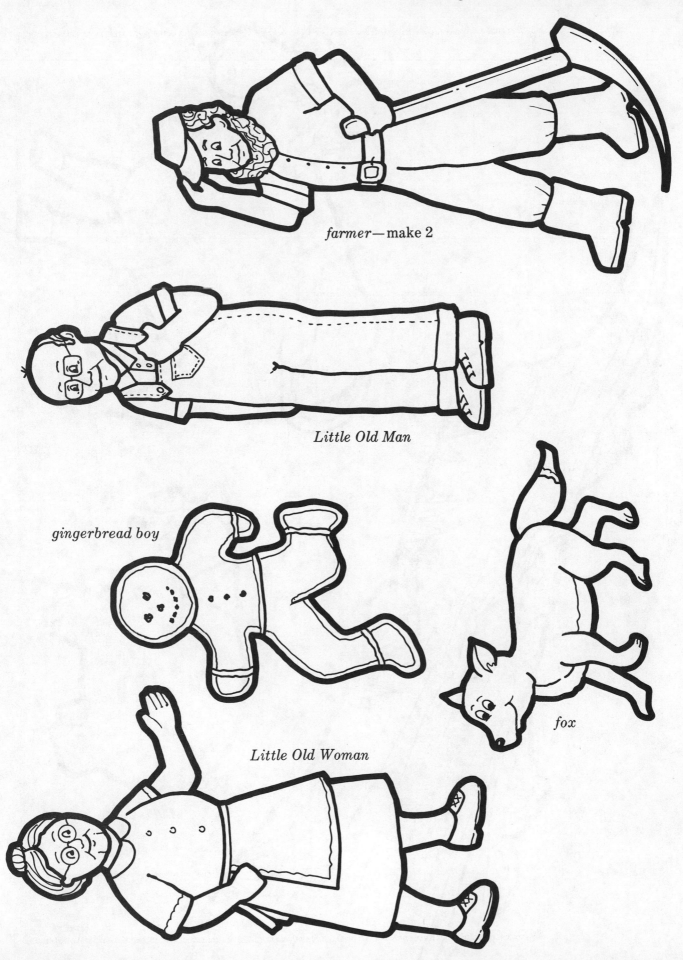

farmer—make 2

Little Old Man

gingerbread boy

fox

Little Old Woman

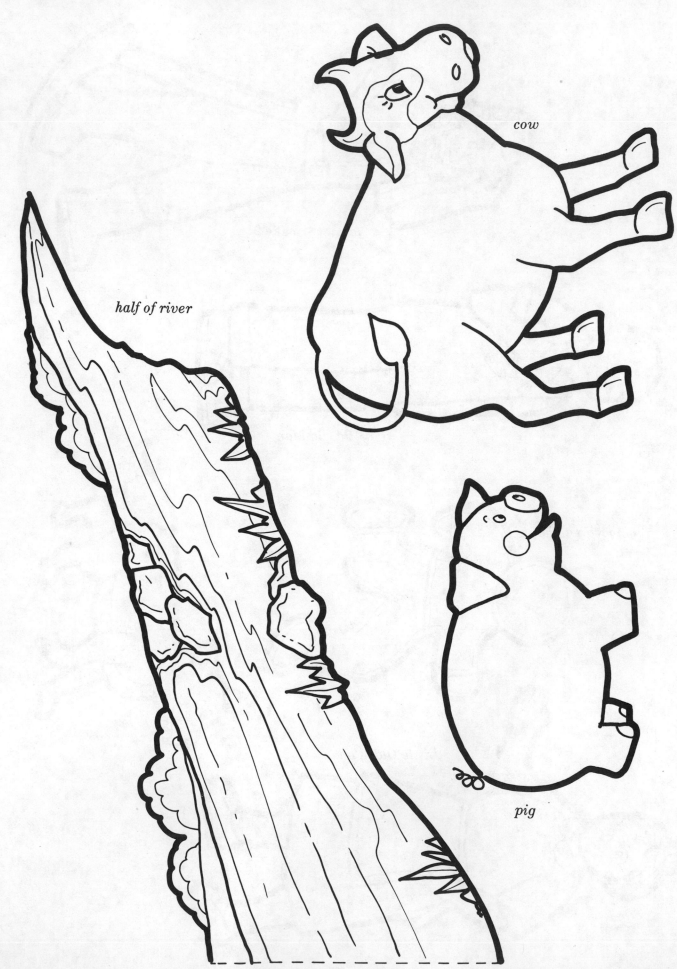

cow

half of river

pig

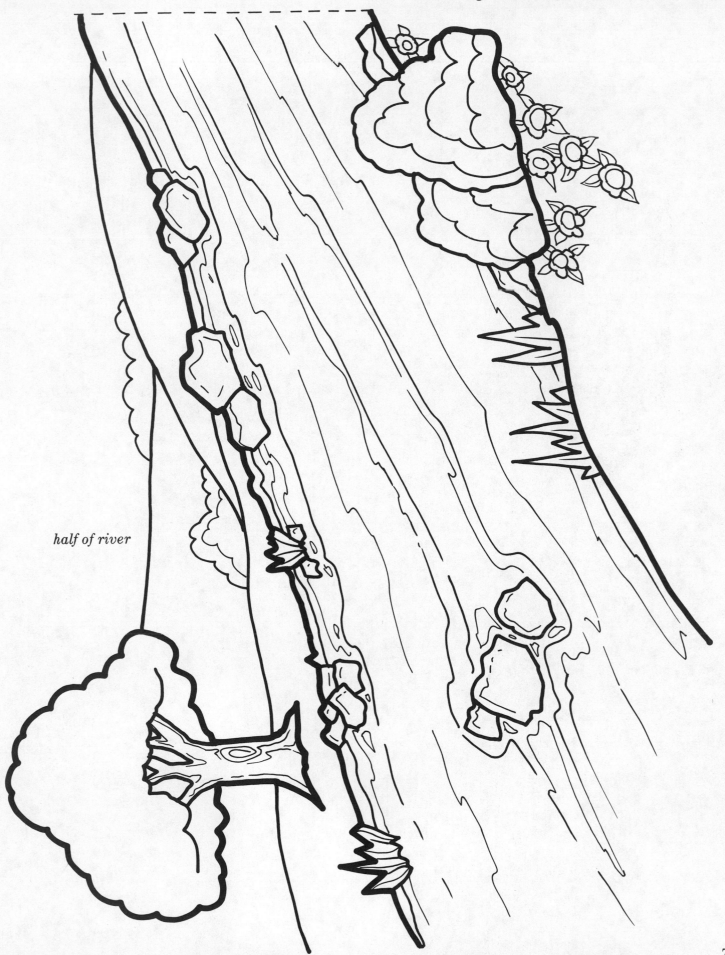

half of river

THE BEAR FAMILY ADVENTURES

The Adventures of Calico Bear

Andrew was gathering bright colored autumn leaves from under the trees when he heard his grandmother call, "Andrew, Andrew, I'm home. Come and see what I've brought you from Uncle Charlie's flea market."

Andrew hurried toward the log cabin as fast as he could. Grandmother always had wonderful surprises. Since she had come to live with Andrew and his father, grandmother had made Andrew very happy.

Andrew found his grandmother putting jars of homemade strawberry jam on the pantry shelf. "Amelia Jo Beasley was selling her jam at the flea market. I just couldn't resist buying a few jars; her jam is the best in the county," grandmother said. "Oh, look over here at what Uncle Charlie bought for you. Now where did it go to? Oh, here it is."

Grandmother held up a small honey-colored bear with a bright calico bow around its neck. "Now isn't that just the most adorable little bear you ever have seen, Andrew? Just look at those little button eyes and that sweet little smile. Uncle Charlie said he bought the little bear from a lady in a big mansion south of here. She was selling some of the things from the mansion so she could raise money to fix it up and make it a museum. Uncle Charlie just knew you'd like this little bear for a friend. Now, what do you think of it?" grandmother asked.

"Oh, it's a great bear, grandmother," replied Andrew. "I'll take it with me when I play in the forest."

"That's all well and good," said grandmother, "but mind you don't get the bear all dirty, now. And come in and eat your lunch before you go out to play again."

Andrew sat at the table and began eating a sandwich made with his grandmother's homemade peanut butter and Amelia Jo Beasley's strawberry jam. "Isn't father coming to lunch?" asked Andrew.

"Oh, you know your father," replied grandmother. "He's in his pottery workshop and he won't even remember to eat unless I take him his lunch, which I expect I better do right now. Now you finish up your lunch and then you can go out to play. But mind you don't go too far, now." And grandmother went to take father his lunch.

Andrew gulped down his lunch, picked up the Calico Bear, and headed back towards the forest. He went back to the pile of leaves he had been gathering. He kept picking up leaves until he had a pile big enough to jump into. Calico Bear sat under a tree nearby and watched Andrew.

Andrew loved playing out-of-doors in the shadows of the misty mountains. He loved the trees, the animals, the streams, the big smooth rocks, and he especially loved jumping into piles of crunchy autumn leaves. Andrew got a running start and landed giggling and laughing as the big pile of leaves scattered around him.

"That looks like fun! Please, may I have a turn to jump?" asked the Calico Bear.

"What? Did you say something?" Andrew asked, staring in amazement at the little bear sitting under the tree.

"Yes, of course I did," replied Calico Bear. "I asked to have a turn jumping in the leaves. I haven't had much exercise lately and that looks so exciting."

"Well, it is fun!" replied Andrew. "But, well, if you can talk, can you tell me your name?"

"Oh, of course. My name is Calico Bear. I'm very pleased to meet you," said the bear.

"Yes, I'm glad to meet you, too," replied Andrew. "I'll give you a turn at jumping now. Oh, are you a boy bear or a girl bear?"

"Why do you ask?" said Calico Bear.

"Well, if you're a girl bear you might not want to get your fur messed up by jumping in the leaves the way I do," announced Andrew.

"Don't be silly!" said Calico Bear. "I am a girl bear, but you should know that girl bears can do anything boy bears can do. I love getting my fur messed up when I'm having a good time.

"Oh, I'm glad you like to play. I've been wishing for someone to play with and we'll be good friends and I'll take you everywhere with me," Andrew said.

Andrew and Calico Bear were having a wonderful time jumping in the leaf pile when suddenly they heard a crying noise. "Listen," said Andrew, "it sounds like someone's hurt." "Yes," said Calico Bear, "let's go see who it is. It sounds like the crying is coming from that direction."

So Andrew and Calico Bear headed in the direction of the crying. Before long, they found a little rabbit caught in a trap. "Oh, please help me," the rabbit cried, "my leg's caught and it hurts terribly."

"Hold on, little rabbit," said Andrew, "we'll get you free." Andrew pulled open the trap while Calico Bear helped take the rabbit's leg out. The leg was cut badly. Calico Bear said, "Andrew, run back to the cabin and bring the first aid kit. Hurry now."

Andrew was back in a jiffy and Calico Bear cleaned and bandaged the rabbit's leg carefully. "Oh, thank you," said the rabbit, "you saved me."

"We were glad to help," said Calico Bear. "By the way, what's your name?"

"Yes, and how did this happen?" asked Andrew. "My father told me that people weren't supposed to hunt or trap here in the forest."

"I'm Rosemary Rabbit," she replied, "and I was hurrying home to feed my children when I stepped into this trap. If you hadn't heard my cries; well, I don't know what would have happened to me and my babies. This forest used to be a safe and peaceful home, but lately I've seen people with guns and traps. Some of my deer and rabbit friends have disappeared."

"That's terrible," said Andrew. "I'll tell my father. Those people should be stopped."

"Now you come along with us and we'll take care of you and your babies until your leg is better." said Calico Bear.

And that is the story of how Andrew and Calico Bear had their first adventure helping the animals of the forest. They cared for Rosemary Rabbit and her babies until she was well. Andrew's father and grandmother helped to catch the people who were hunting and trapping in the forest. The forest was once again a safe place for the animals to live.

Rosemary Rabbit told the other animals that Andrew and Calico Bear were wonderful animal doctors, and from then on all the sick animals came to them for help. Andrew and Calico Bear took care of them all and lived happily in their mountain home.

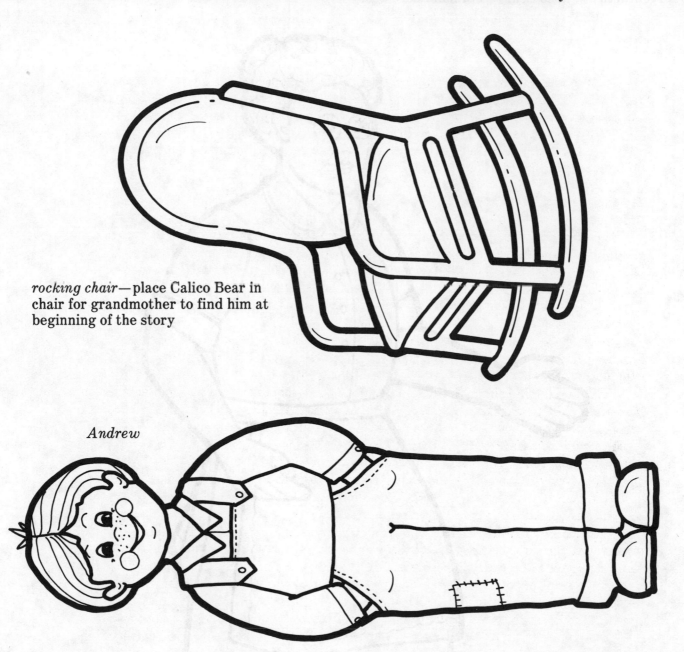

rocking chair—place Calico Bear in chair for grandmother to find him at beginning of the story

Andrew

strawberry jam

Calico Bear

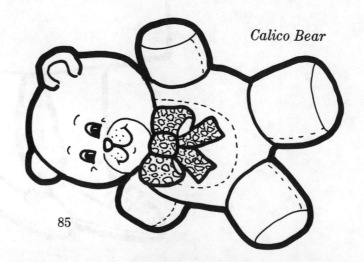

85

grandmother

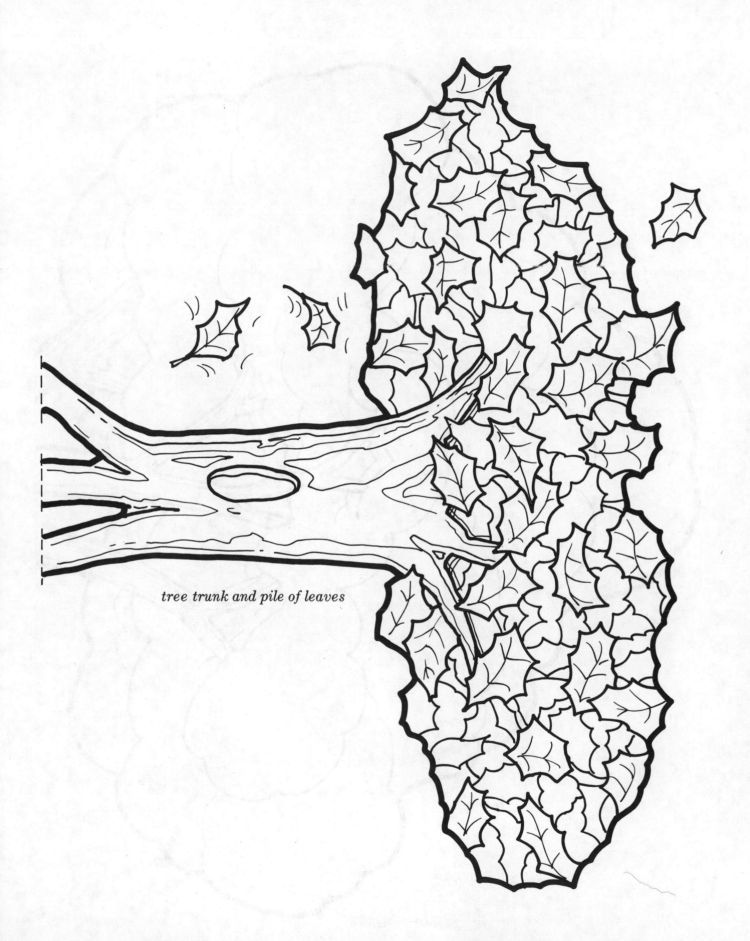

tree trunk and pile of leaves

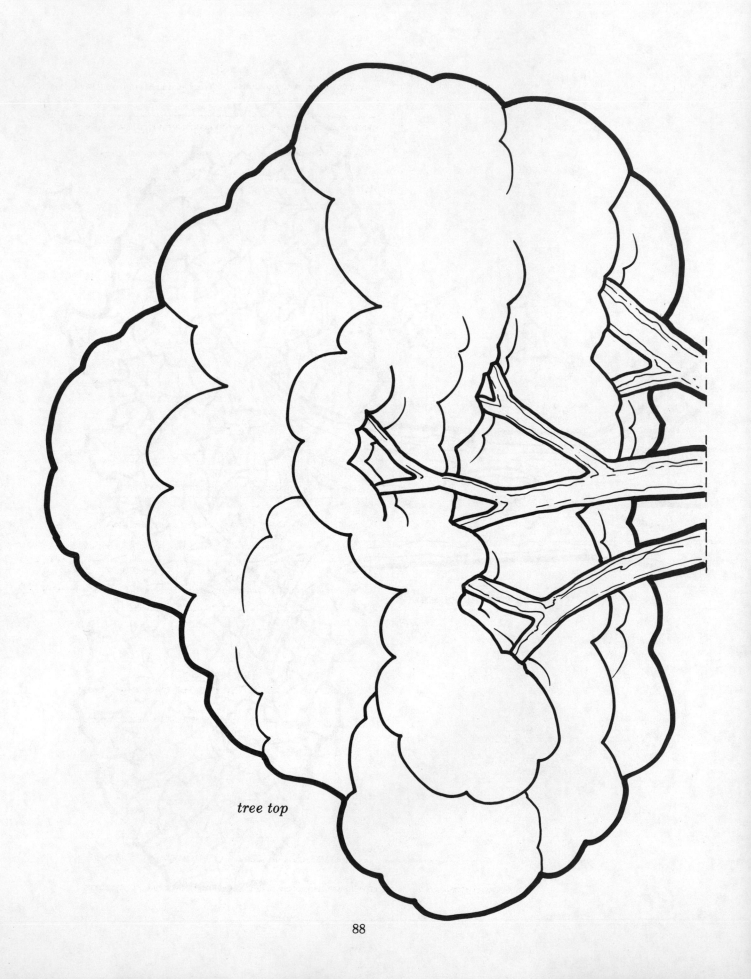

tree top

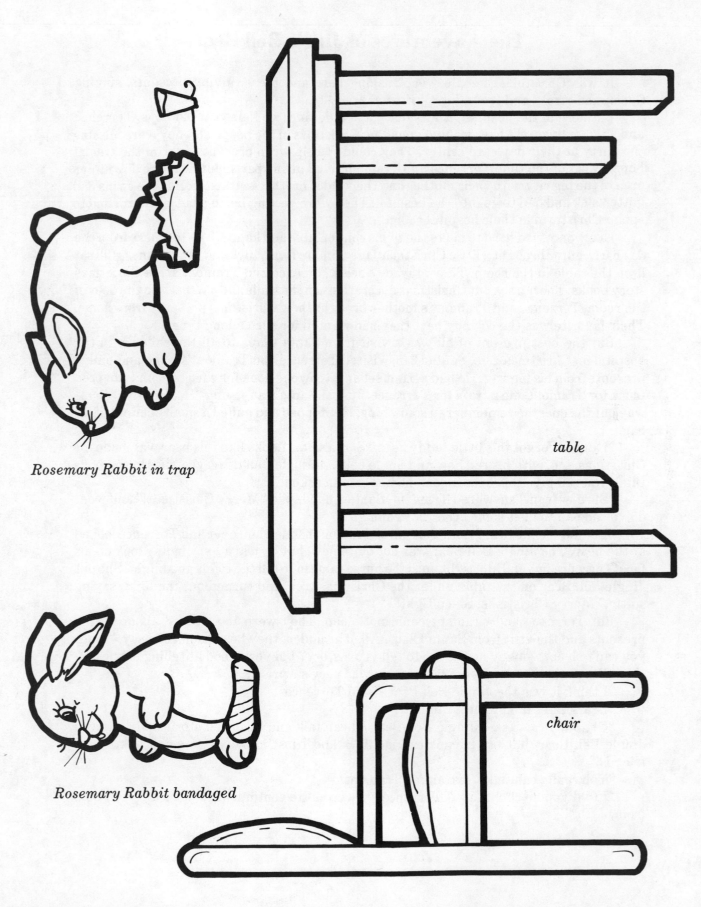

Rosemary Rabbit in trap

table

chair

Rosemary Rabbit bandaged

The Adventures of Jingle Bell Bear

It was Christmas. People were rushing here and there, giving presents, singing Christmas carols, and trimming Christmas trees.

But here in the hospital, it was quiet; too quiet for two four year-old boys. Terrence and Tramont weren't happy about spending Christmas in the hospital. They were missing the party at their day care center. They couldn't help wrap presents or trim the tree at home. Most of the time Terrence and Tramont lived in an apartment near the downtown area of the big city with their mother and their older brother and sister. But the twins had gotten sick and had to go into the hospital. They were getting better, but they still had to spend Christmas in their hospital room.

Everyone tried hard to make the twins comfortable and happy. The teachers from the day care center brought a little Christmas tree trimmed with toys and candy canes, and sat it on the table in the room. They stayed to read Terrence and Tramont some Christmas story books. The nurses put Christmas decorations on the walls and a wreath on the door of the room. Terrence and Tramont's mother brought their Christmas presents from home. Their favorite was the cowboy hats they had wanted for such a long time.

But the best present of all was a visit from Santa Claus to all the children in the hospital on Christmas Eve. Santa Claus visited Terrence and Tramont's room and pulled presents from his big bag. He had a paint set and a cowboy book for each boy, and a big red truck for Tramont and a train for Terrence. Just as Santa was saying "Ho! Ho! Ho!" on his way out the door, he remembered something. He stopped and pulled a small bear out of his bag.

"I almost forgot this little teddy bear," Santa said. "Looks like this bear was made for Christmas, too, with his red bow and jingle bells. A Jingle Bell Bear, yes, sir. Do you boys think you can give this bear a good home?" Santa asked."

"Sure we can," answered Tramont. Santa smiled, said "Merry Christmas!" and went down the hall to visit some other boys and girls.

"Let me see the bear," said Terrence. Tramont handed him over and Terrence looked at the bear. The Jingle Bell Bear was not quite new, but he had a very happy look on his face. Terrence hugged him tight until the nurse came in to tell the twins goodnight. She put Jingle Bell Bear on the table under the Christmas tree, and turned out the light, saying softly, "Merry Christmas! Sleep tight!"

But Terrence and Tramont could not sleep. They were too excited about all the presents and the visit from Santa Claus. All of a sudden, they heard someone say, "Since you can't sleep, would you like me to tell you a story? I'm very good at telling stories."

"Who said that?" asked Tramont. He was very surprised.

"I think it was the Jingle Bell Bear!" said Terrence.

"Bears can't talk," said Tramont.

"Oh, but I can," said Jingle Bell Bear. "I can talk and I can tell stories. My name is Jingle Bell Bear, but my friends call me J. B. and I just know we're going to be good friends."

"You really can talk," exclaimed Tramont.

"I told you he could talk," Terrence answered. He continued, "Where did you come from, J. B.?"

"Oh, that's a long story, so I'll tell you just a little about myself. I was born in a big mansion where I lived with my mother and sisters. We were all very happy. I was the favorite of one of the children in the family, but the children grew up and moved away, and their mother gave me to her little granddaughter. This last year I have lived with the little girl—she's very kind—and this Christmas she decided to give some of her toys to the children that had to spend Christmas in the hospital. So that's how I came to be here."

"Wow!" said Tramont, "you're a long way from home."

"Yes," said J. B., "but now my home will be with you, if you'll take good care of me."

"Oh, we will, we will," promised Terrence and Tramont together.

"That's great," smiled J. B. Bear, "and I'll tell you wonderful stories. I used to tell stories to my sisters every night before bedtime."

"We like stories," said Terrence. "Will you tell us one now, J. B.?"

"Sure," replied J. B. Bear. "You boys must be tired and the nurse said you should rest, so close your eyes and I'll tell you a story while you go to sleep."

Version 1 Ending

And there, sitting under the small Christmas tree, J. B. Bear began to tell the twins a story. He told them about a Christmas long, long ago, and about a child who was born in a manger under a bright star, a child who was born to teach the world that all people could live in peace and love.

J. B. Bear told the first Christmas story to Terrence and Tramont and he watched over them as they slept through the night. It had turned out to be a very special Christmas for the twins, thanks to a small Christmas bear called J. B.

Version 2 Ending

And there, sitting under the small Christmas tree, J. B. Bear began to tell the twins a story, and as J. B. talked, the boys drifted off to sleep.

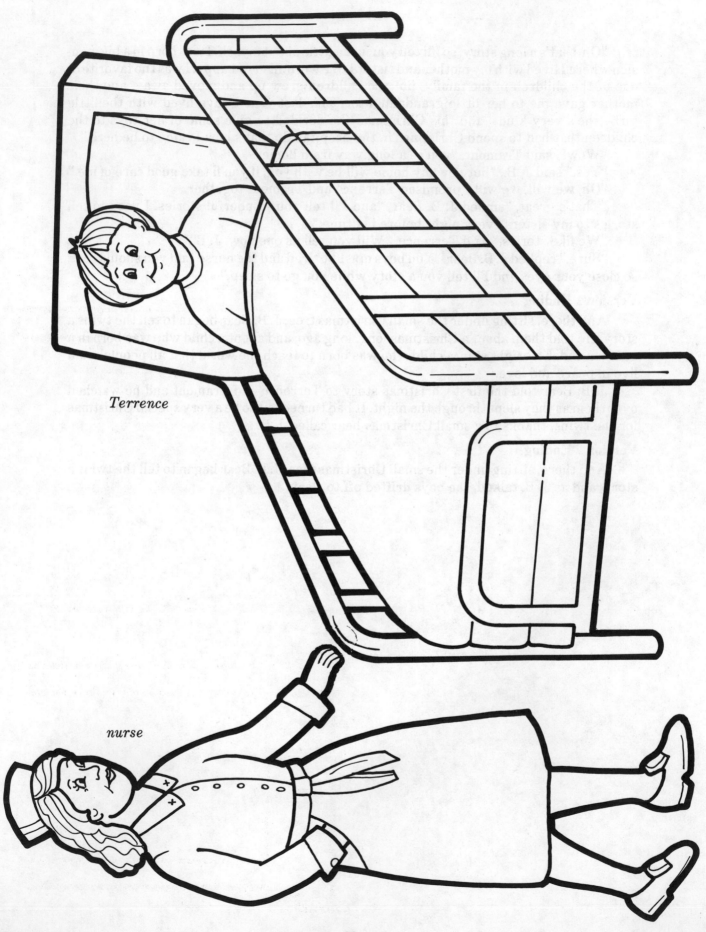

Terrence

nurse

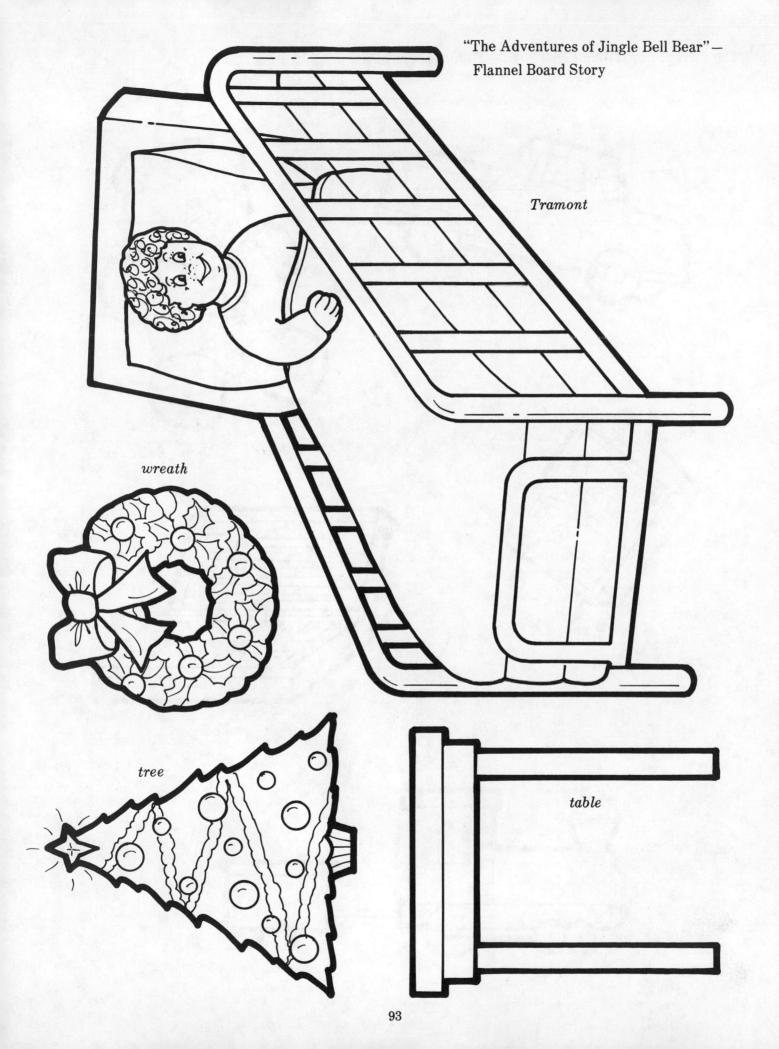

"The Adventures of Jingle Bell Bear"—
Flannel Board Story

Tramont

wreath

tree

table

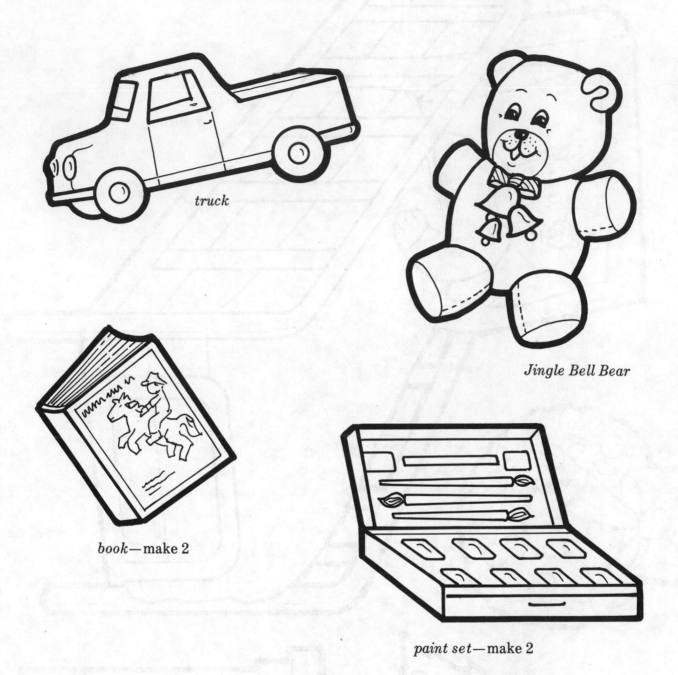

truck

Jingle Bell Bear

book—make 2

paint set—make 2

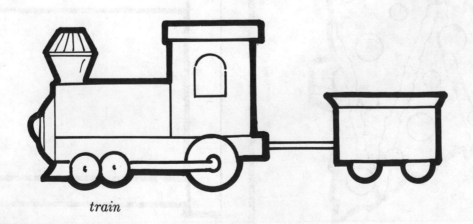

train

Santa Claus

The Adventures of Peppermint Bear

This is the story of a small bear named Peppermint. It all began on a dark, rainy, Spring day. Joshua, Tanya, and Christine were playing in the attic of their big, old house.

Tanya and Christine looked through the trunk full of old clothes, hats, and shoes. They liked to play dress-up on rainy days. Soon Tanya was wearing a big, flowery shawl and Christine was wearing a purple hat and high heeled shoes.

Josh, who was three, watched his older sisters (Tanya was eight and Christine was nine) as he held his own Comfortable Bear and watched the rain hit the attic windows. Then Josh saw a large red handkerchief in the trunk. He decided it would make a great Superman cape, so he reached over to pull it out. When he did, he also pulled out something small, brown, and furry. Joshua, who liked bears very much, got excited when he saw that the furry thing was a small brown bear, with bright button eyes, a happy smile, and a red and white peppermint striped bow around its neck.

"A Peppermint Bear," said Josh as he picked up the small bear and tucked it under his arm. Tanya and Christine came over to look at the Peppermint Bear.

"Why, he looks quite old and wise," said Christine.

"Yes," agreed Tanya, "but why haven't we seen him before when we've played in the trunk?"

"I'm a 'she,'" replied the small bear. "My name is Peppermint Bear. The reason you haven't seen me before is that I just arrived here in the attic. I was tucked away inside an old straw hat that came from your great-grandmother's house. Your great-uncle hid me there one day many years ago, and I've been in the straw hat all this time. Oh, it feels so good to be out in the world again! I haven't talked to anyone but Prickly Penelope for a long time!"

"Who is Prickly Penelope?" asked Christine.

Just then, a little hedgehog came out of the trunk, saying in an angry voice, "My, what a commotion! What is all this noise and excitement, Peppermint?"

Peppermint Bear smiled and explained to the children, "Don't mind Penelope. Hedgehogs can seem grumpy, but they are really very nice animals."

The three children thought that Prickly Penelope did look very grumpy, but because they liked Peppermint Bear so much, they decided to be friendly to Penelope.

Penelope looked at the children, sighed and said, "Well, I suppose you'll have to do. I guess you're here to help us catch the thief."

"Thief? What are you talking about?" asked Tanya.

"Oh my, oh my," sighed Penelope. "What a day this has been. We've been left alone for a long time in the trunk, and just this morning my old friend, Louise Ladybug, flew in to warn us about the thief. How she found us, hidden away in this dusty old trunk, I'll never know, but somehow she did, and . . . oh my, oh my."

"Penelope," said Peppermint Bear, "you haven't finished telling the children about the thief."

"Oh my, oh my, yes, yes, of course. Well, Louise Ladybug came in to warn us about the thief who is going all over town taking children's teddy bears. This makes the children very unhappy. Louise said that Peppermint should keep hiding until someone comes along to catch the thief, and I just supposed that you were the someones who had come to help us!"

"A Teddy Bear Thief!" said Josh. "How awful! I'll catch him!" "Yes, we'll all help," said Christine and Tanya.

"Wonderful. Wonderful." Penelope continued, "You children go and catch the Teddy Bear Thief while Peppermint and I hide here in the trunk until this terrible, terrible thing is over."

"Penelope," laughed Peppermint Bear, "you can hide in the trunk if you like, but I am going to help Christine and Tanya and Josh. We can't send the children out on such an adventure all by themselves."

"Well," said Penelope crossly, "you can help them if you want to. But I am going to stay here in the trunk where it's safe." Penelope ran back into the trunk and hid under the red handkerchief.

At that moment Louise Ladybug flew in through a crack in the window. "Quickly, quickly," she called. "I've just seen the Teddy Bear Thief running down the street!"

The children and Peppermint Bear hurried down the stairs and out the door. The rain had stopped and the children followed Louise Ladybug down the street. Christine and Tanya hurried ahead, but Josh wasn't able to keep up with them. Peppermint Bear, who was tucked tightly under Josh's arm, suddenly said, "There — There he is! I think I saw the thief!"

Josh turned in the direction Peppermint Bear was pointing and said, "Yes, you're right. I do see someone. Let's follow him."

By this time Christine and Tanya were too far ahead to hear him call, so Josh and Peppermint Bear set out after the Teddy Bear Thief on their own. They followed the thief to a house on the corner. Josh looked into a window and saw a big chair covered with teddy bears. Just then, the Teddy Bear Thief tiptoed up behind Josh, grabbed Peppermint Bear, and ran towards the house. Josh ran after him, yelling, "Stop! Stop, you Teddy Bear Thief! Give me back my Peppermint Bear!"

All of a sudden the Teddy Bear Thief stopped and began to cry. "Why are you crying?" demanded Josh. "I'm the one who just lost my teddy bear."

"I know," said the Teddy Bear Thief, "but I can't help it. I never had a teddy bear when I was a little boy and it made me so sad," sniffled the thief, "and that's why I've been taking all the teddy bears and now you've caught me. Please don't be angry with me."

"But I am angry," said Josh. "You have made many children sad."

Peppermint Bear added, "Just because you were a sad child doesn't mean you can make other children sad. Children need their teddy bears to love and cuddle and to talk to. It is not all right to take someone else's teddy bear to make yourself happy."

"I know," said the Teddy Bear Thief, drying his tears. "Anyway, I've been feeling terrible instead of feeling happy. I'm sorry. I'll take all the teddy bears back to the children and tell them all that I'm sorry and I'll never take what doesn't belong to me again."

"Good for you!" said Josh. "We'll help you."

So Josh and Peppermint Bear went to find Christine and Tanya and they all helped the Teddy Bear Thief take the teddy bears back to their homes. All the children in the town were happy.

And the Teddy Bear Thief wasn't a thief anymore. His real name was Arthur, and Christine felt so sorry for him that she gave him one of her teddy bears for his very own. And Arthur has been a good friend to all children and bears to this very day.

As for the children, well, Josh, Tanya, and Christine took Peppermint Bear home and told their parents what had happened. They were all glad the adventure had ended safely.

Peppermint Bear told Prickly Penelope that it was safe to come out of the trunk and they were both taken to live in the playroom along with Comfortable Bear and the other stuffed animals. Louise Ladybug visited the playroom often.

Christine, Tanya, Josh, Peppermint Bear, Prickly Penelope and all the other animals lived happily together.

"The Adventures of Peppermint Bear" — Flannel Board Story

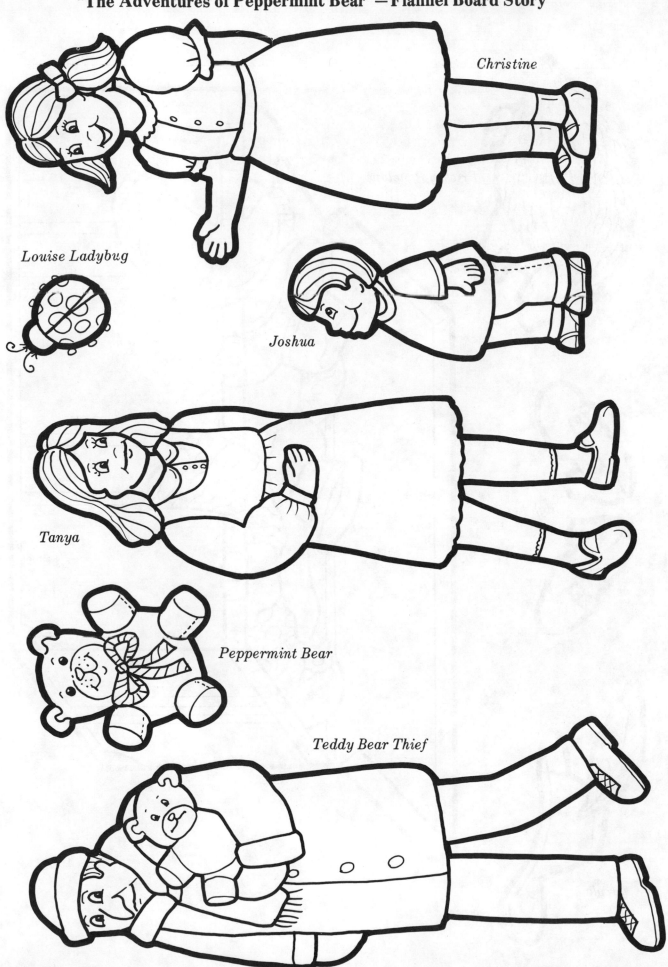

Christine

Louise Ladybug

Joshua

Tanya

Peppermint Bear

Teddy Bear Thief

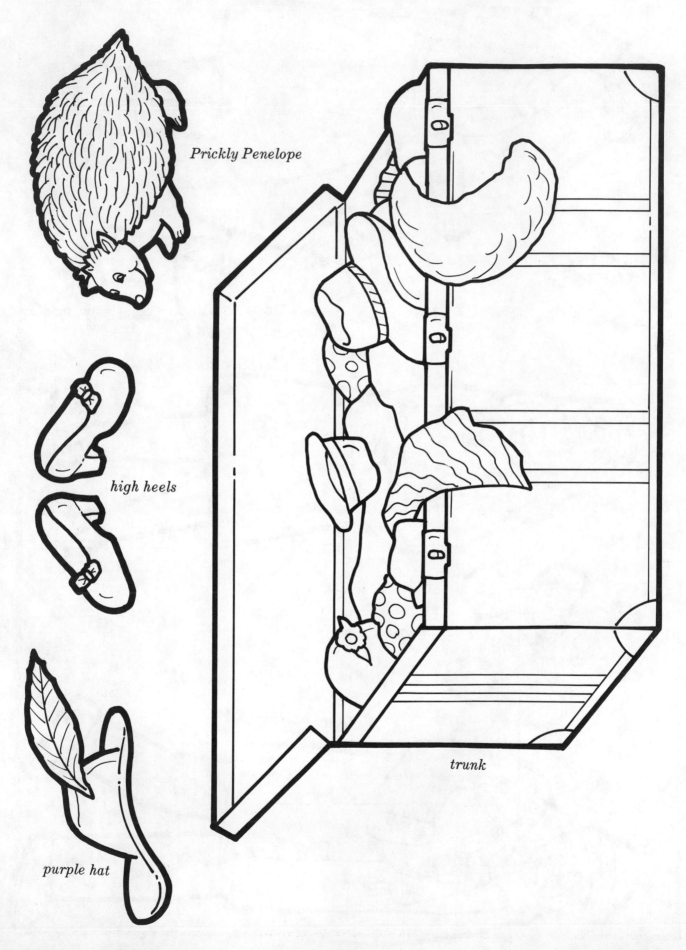

Prickly Penelope

high heels

purple hat

trunk

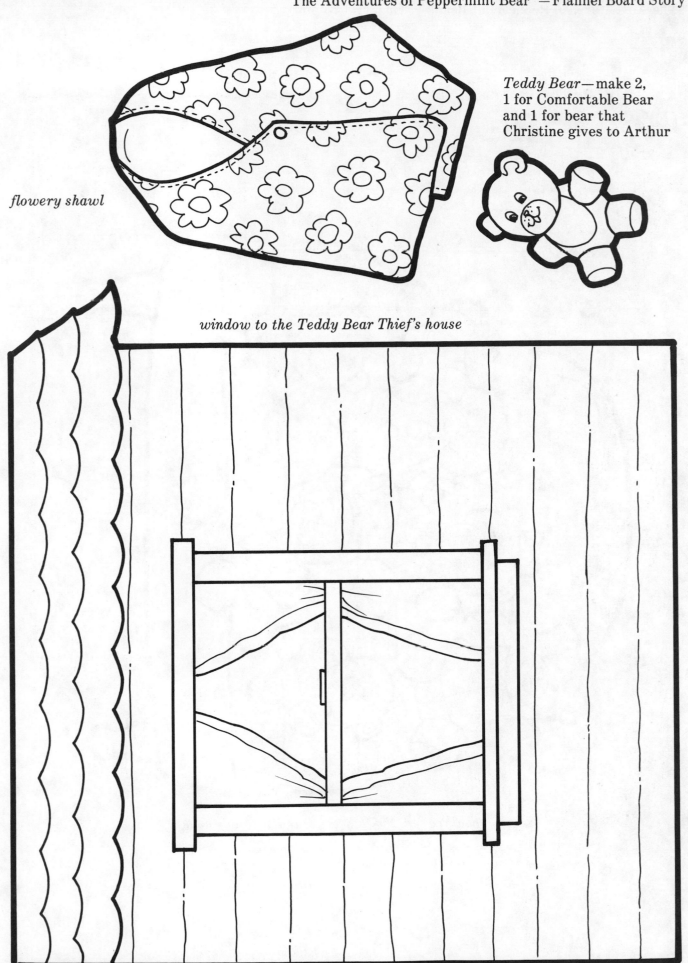

flowery shawl

Teddy Bear—make 2,
1 for Comfortable Bear
and 1 for bear that
Christine gives to Arthur

window to the Teddy Bear Thief's house

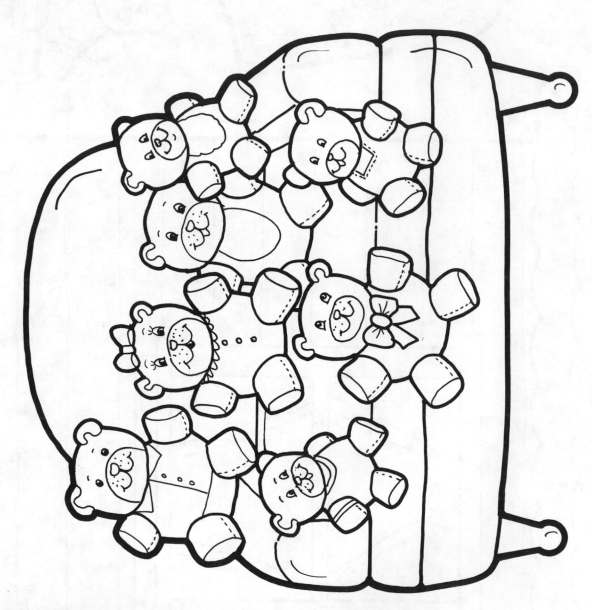

chair covered with bears found at thief's house

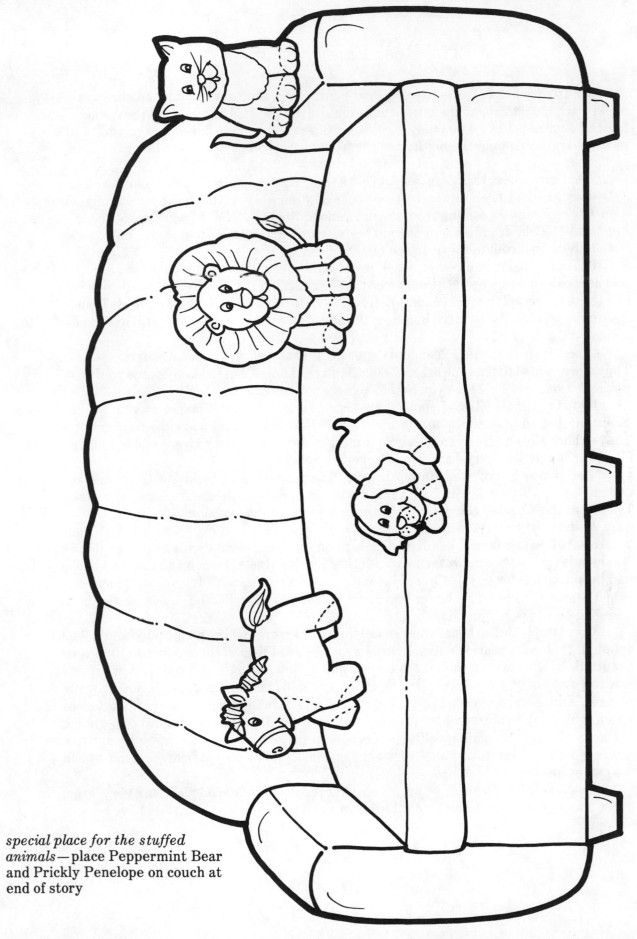

special place for the stuffed animals—place Peppermint Bear and Prickly Penelope on couch at end of story

The Bear Family Reunion

It was so hot that Uncle Elwood Bear's fur was getting very damp and sticky as he walked around outside at the big old mansion. July in the southern part of the country is like that, hot and sticky, and today was the 4th of July. The whole house was getting ready for the parade, hanging the big flag on the front porch, and baking goodies for the family picnic.

What a wonderful July 4th it would be! Estelle Bear was very excited. This was going to be a very special day because her three bear children were coming home for a family reunion. Calico Bear was coming from the mountains, Jingle Bell Bear from the big city, and Peppermint Bear from a small town; they were all going to be together again at last! Estelle Bear just couldn't wait to see her children!

The old mansion had been cleaned from end to end and from top to bottom. It looked just as nice as it had when the bears were little bear cubs. The children were all gone now and the mansion was a museum, but Estelle Bear, Uncle Elwood Bear, and Cousin Louella Bear (who was too shy to leave home for the adventures most bears have) still lived in the mansion.

Calico Bear, Jingle Bell Bear, and Peppermint Bear met each other at the train station. They were so glad to see each other! They all talked at once. "I'm so happy to see you!" "Oh, you look wonderful!" "I love you both!" "Where's mother? I can't wait to see her!"

Just then Uncle Elwood spotted his nieces and nephew and began waving his hat. "Your mother and Cousin Louella are waiting in the car," he said while the bear children hugged him. The children ran to see their mother and cousin. There were still more hugs. The bear family was very happy to be together again.

"Let's hurry home," said Mother Estelle. "I have a wonderful picnic waiting for us, and we can watch the big 4th of July parade when it goes past the house." So, with Uncle Elwood at the wheel of the old car, the bears set out for the mansion.

Waiting for them was the grandest 4th of July picnic you ever saw: fried chicken, potato salad, baked beans, deviled eggs, corn on the cob, biscuits with honey, apple pie, homemade ice cream, and watermelon. Mother Estelle, Uncle Elwood and Cousin Louella had been cooking for days! "Cousin Louella, Cousin Louella, don't forget the lemonade," called Uncle Elwood. The bears had their picnic and enjoyed the music as the band marched by in the big parade.

After the picnic the bears were so full they just sat around the picnic table and talked about all their adventures. Calico Bear began, "Where I live, in the mountains, it is very beautiful. In the autumn the leaves turn bright yellow, orange, and red, and my friend Andrew and I play in the leaves. In the winter the snow falls and makes a beautiful white blanket. Andrew and I go sledding down the mountain. In the spring everything becomes green again, and Andrew and I plant a garden. And summer is lazy and fun. We go wading in the creek and play games with the animals in the forest. I am so happy living with Andrew in the mountains." Mother Estelle Bear said, "What a wonderful life it must be in the mountains."

Then Jingle Bell Bear spoke up, "Well, I live in a most wonderful place, in a very large, important city. My twins and I ride the city bus and I have been to the zoo. I have been to school, and I have visited a hospital. Once when I was lost, I even had a ride in a police car. I have had many exciting adventures," said Jingle Bell Bear. "Oh, what an exciting life you must live," said Mother Estelle Bear.

The bear children were starting to get jealous of each other. They each wanted Mother Estelle, Uncle Elwood, and Cousin Louella to think that they had the nicest home.

It was Peppermint Bear's turn to tell her story. "I just happen to have some pictures with me," she said. "This is a picture of the big old house I live in, and this is my family. Christine, Tanya and Joshua are the children who care for me. Their mother is a lawyer and their father is a teacher at the university. And this is my room, the playroom."

"Well," said Calico Bear, "the log cabin where I live was built by my family's father. He is a very talented man; he builds houses and furniture and he makes pottery. And the grandmother makes beautiful quilts; she won first prize for quilting at the fair this spring."

Jingle Bell Bear said, "The mother of my twins is a nurse in a very large city hospital. She helps people who are sick every day. And the older brother is a very good musician and he plays in a popular band."

"Oh, dear," thought Mother Estelle Bear, "this is too bad! My children are jealous of each other. They aren't happy for each other as I had hoped they would be."

"Well, mother, what do you think? Which of us has the nicest home?" asked Peppermint Bear. "Yes, mother, tell us," said Calico Bear. "Oh, but I live in a big important city. You can see that I have the best home," said Jingle Bell Bear. And the bear children began to argue.

"Now, children, stop this arguing," said Estelle Bear. "You must see that you live in three very different places and it is no good to try to decide if one is better than the other. Each of you has a special home and I am very happy to know that. You must realize that you are very lucky to be loved and cared for by some very special children."

Calico Bear, Jingle Bell Bear, and Peppermint Bear became very quiet. They realized their mother's words were very smart and that they had been very silly to argue. Peppermint Bear spoke first, "Oh, I'm sorry for being so silly. I'm very happy for all of us and I'm so glad we're together today."

"Yes," said Calico Bear, "let's not argue anymore."

"Let's hear more stories," added Jingle Bell Bear.

So the Bear Family talked into the evening, and then they watched the town's fireworks display. It had been a wonderful July 4th and a very special reunion. Before the day was over, the bear family—Mother Estelle, Uncle Elwood, Cousin Louella, Calico Bear, Jingle Bell Bear, and Peppermint Bear—were all making plans for the next year's bear family reunion.

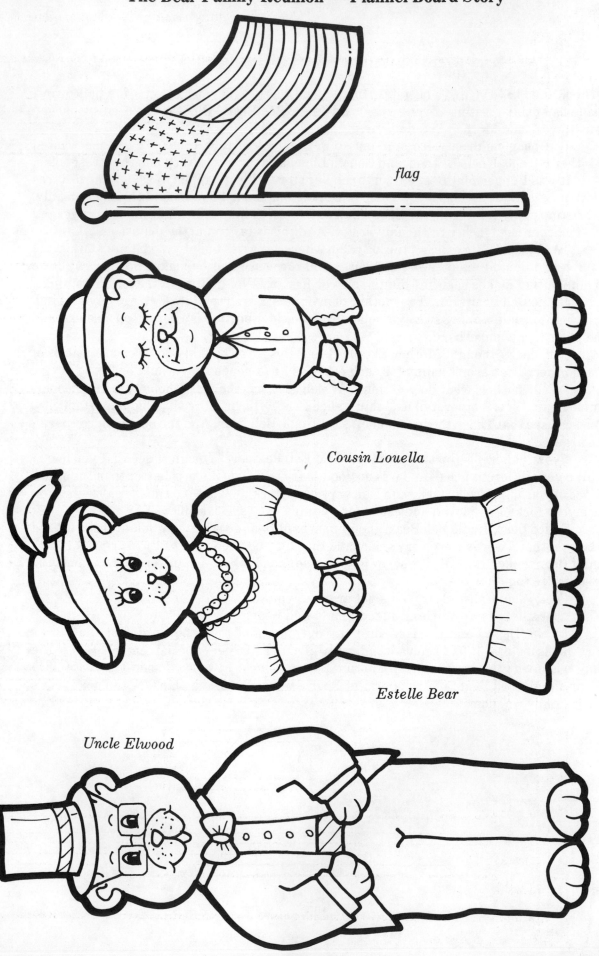

flag

Cousin Louella

Estelle Bear

Uncle Elwood

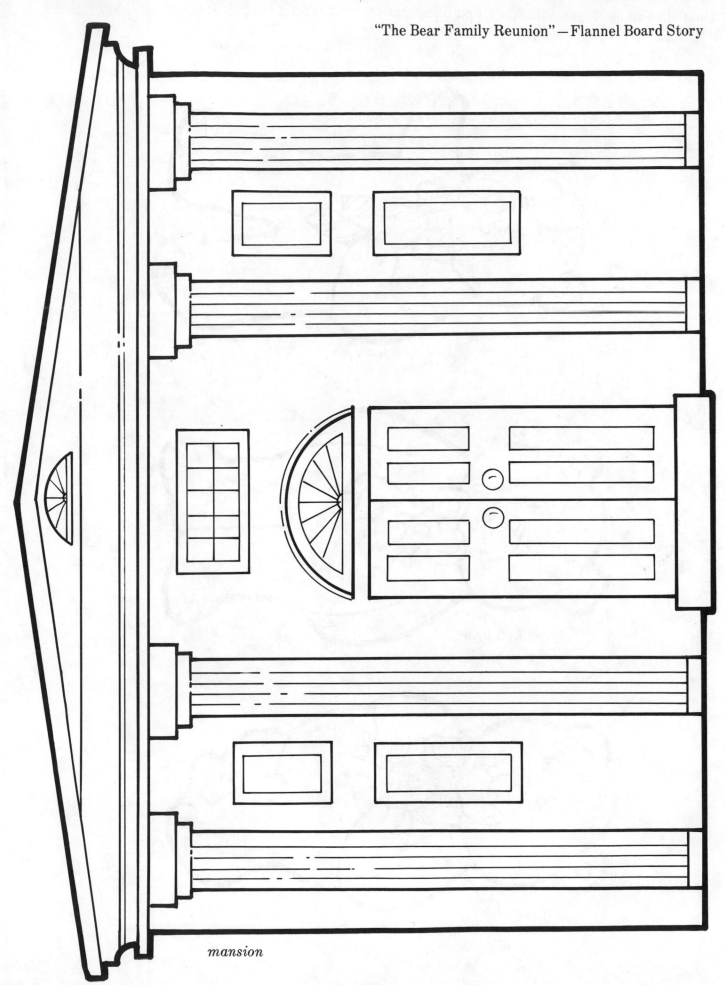

mansion

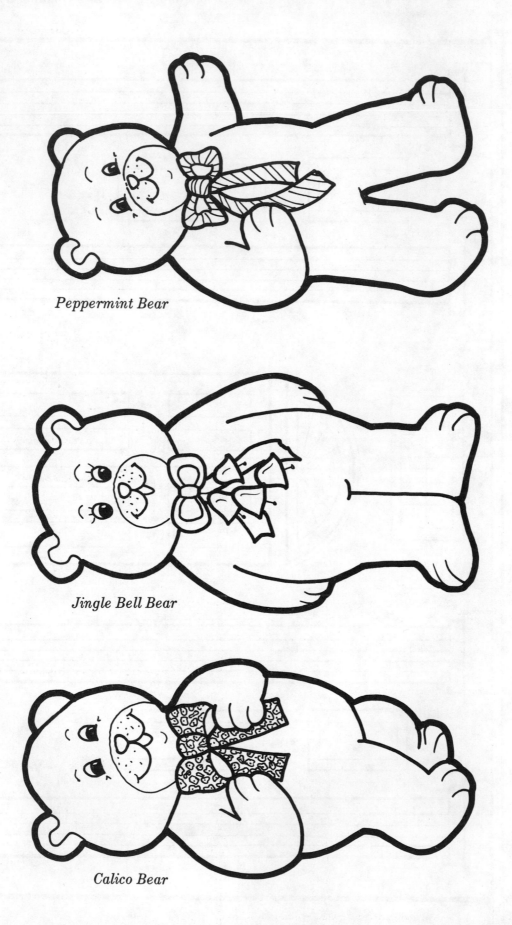

Peppermint Bear

Jingle Bell Bear

Calico Bear

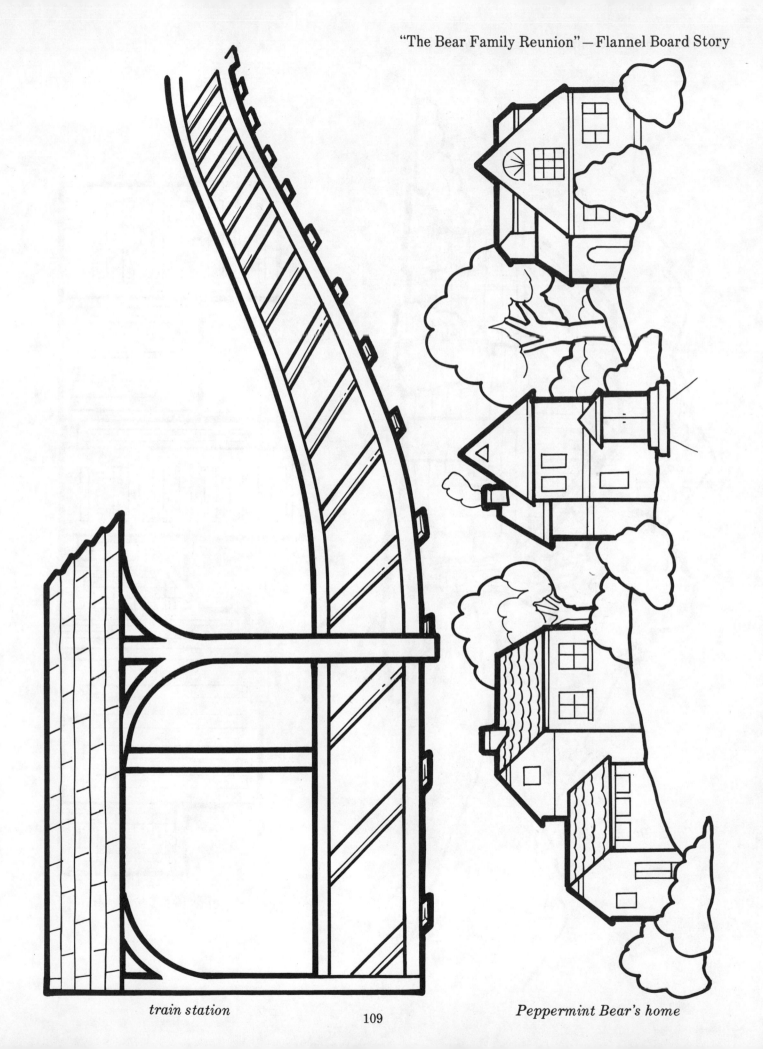

train station

Peppermint Bear's home

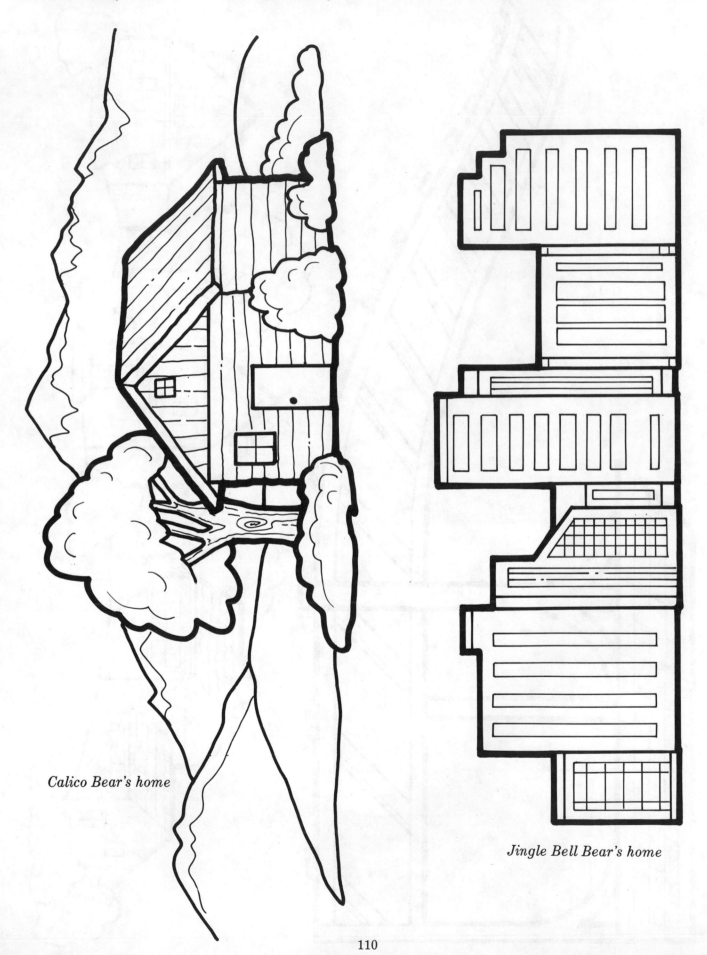

Calico Bear's home

Jingle Bell Bear's home

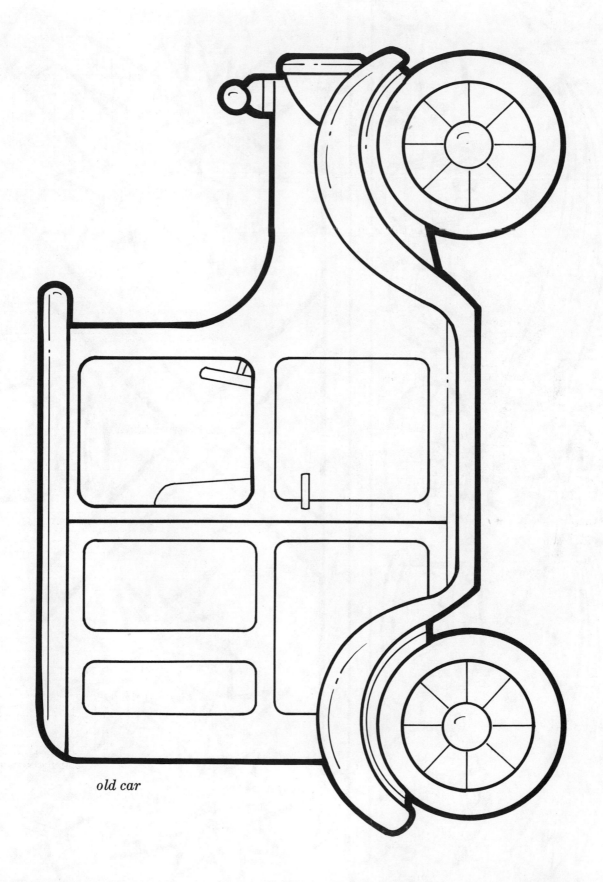

old car

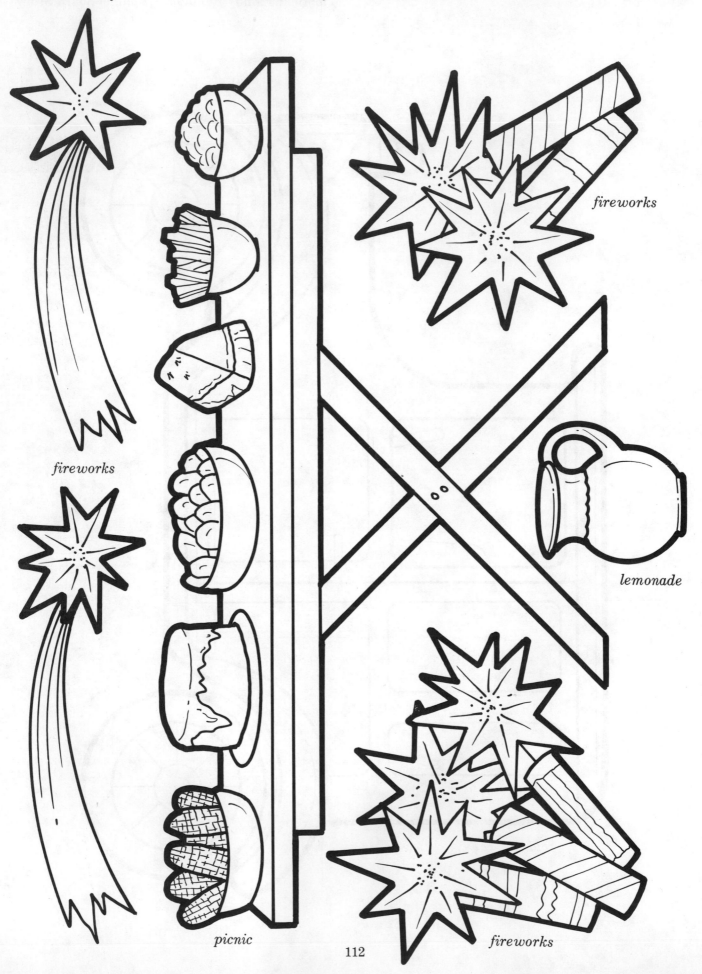

fireworks

fireworks

fireworks

lemonade

picnic

fireworks

ANIMAL TALES

Gus the Runaway Guinea Pig

It was raining. Rodney and Steven were playing with blocks in their kindergarten classroom. They had made a tower, a road, and a bridge, and now they were making a house for Gus the Guinea Pig.

Every day the children in the class got their friend Gus out of his cage so he could run around and play. Now Gus was playing in the big block house that Rodney and Steven had made for him.

Suddenly it was raining harder. There was lightning and thunder. The children ran to the windows to watch the lightning crackle in the sky. The teacher told them that they were safe from the storm and everyone went back to play.

"Oh, no," shrieked Rodney, "Gus is gone!"

"Gus is a runaway!" cried Steven.

"Maybe the rain and thunder frightened him," suggested the teacher. "Let's look for him. He must be nearby."

They looked under the rocking chair.

But Gus wasn't there.

They looked behind the cabinet.

But Gus wasn't there.

They looked under the easel.

But Gus wasn't there.

They looked in the closet.

But Gus wasn't there.

They looked under the table.

But Gus wasn't there.

They looked on the shelf.

But Gus wasn't there.

Just as they were about to give up, Steven heard a squeaking sound coming from the playhouse. And there, sitting in the doll bed with Raggedy Ann, was Gus the Runaway Guinea Pig.

"Oh, Gus, we thought you were lost forever," said Rodney.

"We're so glad to see you, Gus," said Steven, giving Gus a squeeze.

"I think Gus has had enough excitement for one day," said the teacher. "Let's put him back in his house now."

So Rodney and Steven put Gus back in his cage and gave him some lettuce as an extra treat.

A tired Gus the Guinea Pig nibbled his lettuce and settled down to take a nap. He was glad he wasn't a runaway anymore.

Gus

lettuce

teacher

116

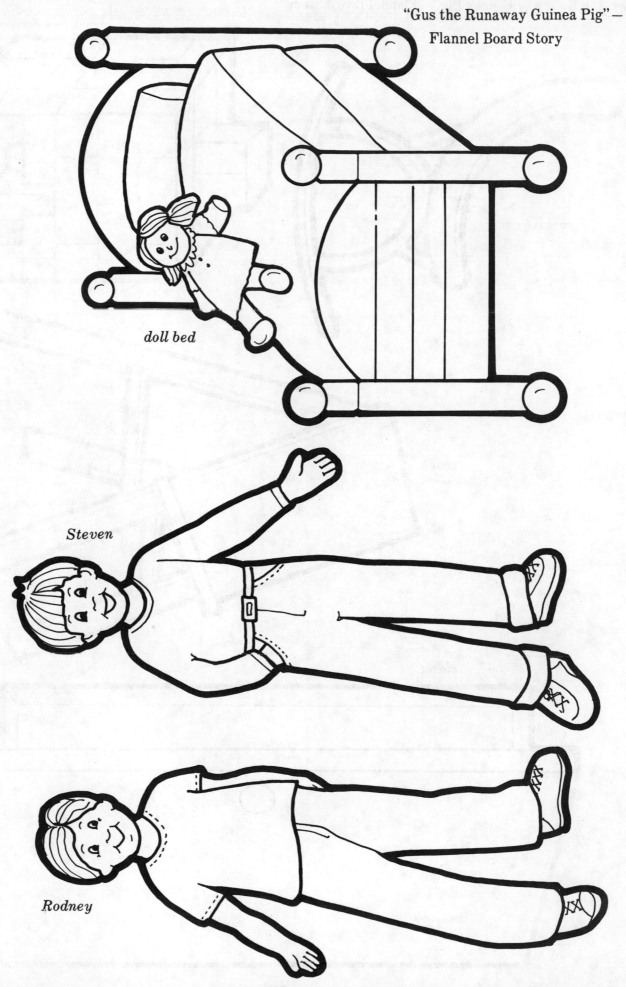

doll bed

Steven

Rodney

block house

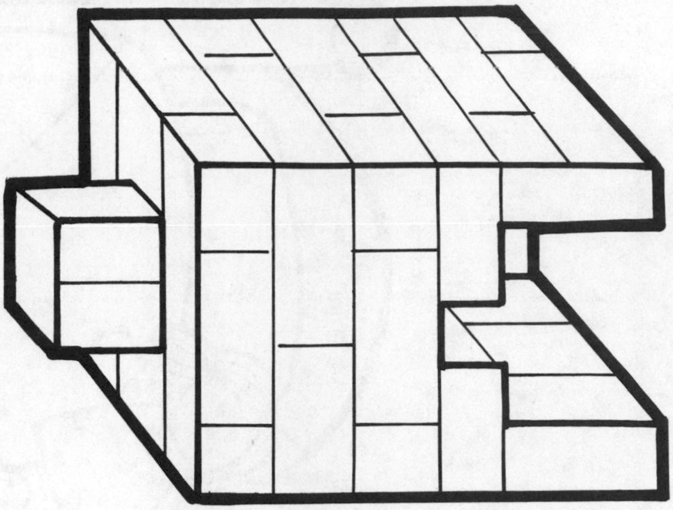

rocking chair

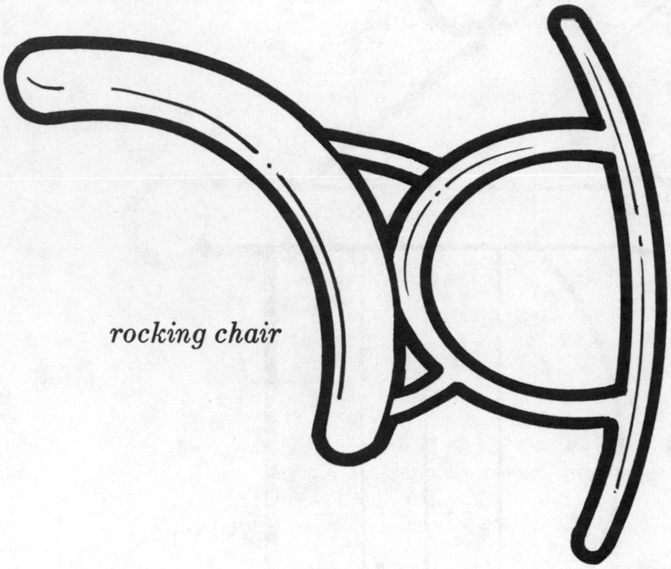

easel

closet

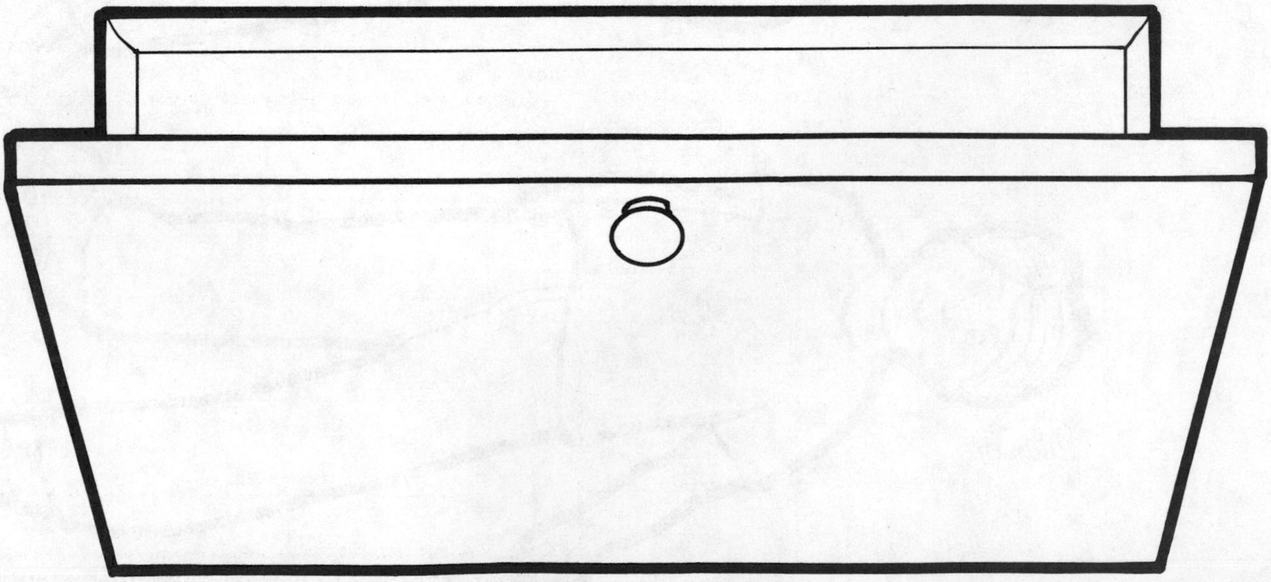

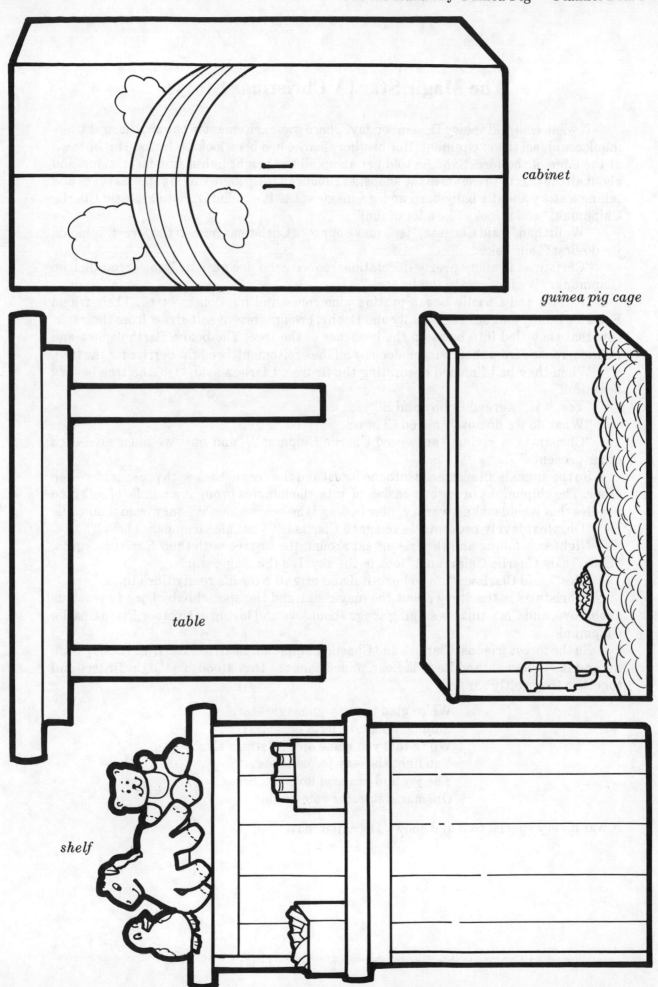

cabinet

guinea pig cage

table

shelf

The Magic Star (A Christmas Story)

It was a cold and snowy December day. There was excitement in the air. Clarissa Chipmunk could feel the excitement. Her brother Charlie had been looking for food in the town at the edge of the forest and he told her about all the bright lights and decorations, and about all the pretty presents in the shops, and about all the people singing special songs and telling a story about a baby born under a magic star. "It's called Christmas," said Charlie Chipmunk, "and it looks like a lot of fun!"

"Well, then," said Clarissa, "let's make our own Christmas here in the forest. What do we do first?" she asked.

"Christmas is many pretty decorations, so we need decorations," answered Charlie Chipmunk. "We'll decorate the fir tree."

Clarissa and Charlie began putting pine cones and nuts on the tree. Their friend Beatrice Bunny and her twins, Billy and Bobby, brought bits of soft straw from their burrow that they tied into bows on the branches of the tree. The bears, Bartholomew and Belinda, roused from their winter sleep by all the excitement, brought berries for the tree.

When they had finished decorating the fir tree, Clarissa said, "Oh, the tree is very beautiful!"

"Yes, it is," agreed Bobby and Billy.

"What do we do now?" asked Clarissa.

"Christmas is giving," answered Charlie Chipmunk, "and now we must give each other presents."

So the animals all scattered into the forest and they came back with presents for each other. The chipmunks brought a basket of nuts, the bunnies brought a bundle of soft pine needles that would make a warm winter bed, and the bears brought honey from their cave.

"Oh, what lovely presents!" exclaimed Clarissa. "What nice friends we have!"

Night was falling and the friends sat around the fir tree with their Christmas gifts. "Look," said Charlie Chipmunk, "look in the sky! It's the magic star!"

"Yes," said Clarissa, "it's so beautiful and bright! Now it's really Christmas!"

"Christmas is the story about the magic star and the special baby born to teach us about love, and Christmas is singing songs about love and loving each other," said Charlie Chipmunk.

So the forest friends, Clarissa and Charlie Chipmunk, Beatrice, Billy, and Bobby Bunny, and Bartholomew and Belinda Bear, joined hands as they stood around the fir tree and together they softly sang:

> We're glad to see you, magic star,
> Shining up above from oh-so-far!
> We're told you shine on Christmas Eve,
> You light the way for us to see,
> The joy and peace of love you bring,
> Oh, magic star, for you we sing.

It was a very special cold and snowy December day.

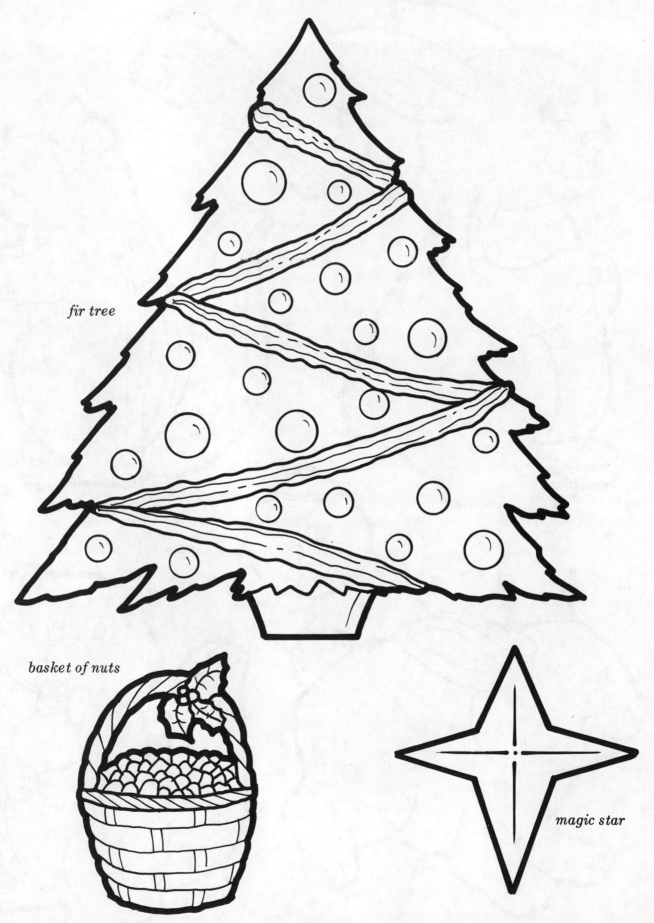

fir tree

basket of nuts

magic star

"The Magic Star"—Flannel Board Story

pine needles

Clarissa Chipmunk

Beatrice Bunny

HONEY

honey

Charlie Chipmunk

bunny—make 2 for Billy and Bobby

122

Belinda Bear

Bartholomew Bear

The Peaceable Kingdom

This is the story of a kingdom where many different kinds of animals live together in harmony. There is a legend that tells the story of how the animals left their old home where there was much war and much fighting, to look for a new home where they could live in peace.

The story begins:

They came to live on the mountaintop, many years ago.
The legend says they came in peace, looking for a home where love could grow.

And so they all came together — the giraffe, the lion, the bear, the lamb, the chipmunk, the cow, the monkey, the dog, the cat, and the deer. They were led by the beautiful unicorn to the green and growing mountain top. This is where they made their home.

The animals believed it was important to learn to live together in happiness and peace. They cared for each other and worked together and created a beautiful new home.

They learned that feelings are important and decided that each animal would have the responsibility of teaching a special feeling to the younger animals so that the young ones would learn to respect feelings as they grew up.

The giraffe was given sadness.
The lion was given bravery.
The bear was given thoughtfulness.
The lamb was given peace.
The chipmunk was given fear.
The cow was given acceptance.
The monkey was given anger.
The dog was given happiness.
The cat was given jealousy.
The deer was given tenderness.
The unicorn was given love.

The animals taught all the different feelings so that the young ones would not be frightened of any of their feelings, but would learn to accept all of their feelings as a part of life. The unicorn helped the young ones to understand the importance of love, and the bear taught the young ones that their loving, tender, peaceful feelings were the most special ones.

So all the different kinds of animals lived in harmony on their mountain top. Their story was a happy one.

They came to live on the mountain top, many years ago.
The legend says they came in peace, looking for a home where love could grow.

A discussion of feelings is a good accompaniment to this story. Use pictures of people expressing a variety of feelings to help children identify feelings they have experienced.

bear

giraffe

cat

chipmunk

lion

lamb

cow

monkey

dog

unicorn

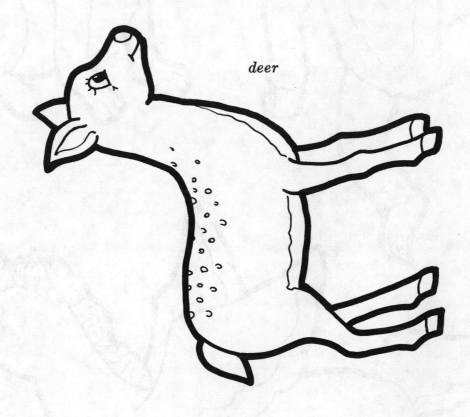

deer

The Journey to the Picnic Rock

It was time. In the forest the signs of Spring were everywhere — trees were budding, flowers were blooming, and baby animals were playing in the sunshine. It was definitely time for a picnic, and a picnic meant a journey to the picnic rock. The picnic rock was a special place for the animals in the forest. The big flat rock was perched at the edge of the rocky stream and was a perfect spot for a picnic.

The first picnic of the Spring was always the most special one. Today Sammy Squirrel decided to invite his best friend, Rebecca Rabbit, to go to the picnic rock for their very first picnic of the year. The two friends hurried to get ready for the picnic. Sammy brought the picnic basket and Rebecca brought the jug of lemonade. They started on their journey to the picnic rock.

They hadn't gone far when they passed Roscoe Raccoon. Roscoe saw the picnic basket and said, "Oh, I just love picnics. The day is perfect for the first Spring picnic. May I come along?" "Of course, please join us," replied the friendly squirrel. So Sammy Squirrel, Rebecca Rabbit, and Roscoe Raccoon continued on their journey to the picnic rock.

They hadn't gone much further when they passed Dorothy Deer. Dorothy saw the picnic basket and said, "Oh, I just love picnics. The day is perfect for the first Spring picnic. May I come along?" "Of course, please join us," replied the friendly squirrel. So Sammy Squirrel, Rebecca Rabbit, Roscoe Raccoon, and Dorothy Deer continued on their journey to the picnic rock.

They hadn't gone much farther when they passed Benjamin Bear. Benjamin saw the picnic basket and said, "Oh, I just love picnics. The day is perfect for the first Spring picnic. May I come along?" "Of course, please join us," replied the friendly squirrel. So Sammy Squirrel, Rebecca Rabbit, Roscoe Raccoon, Dorothy Deer, and Benjamin Bear continued on their journey to the picnic rock.

"We certainly are collecting quite a crowd!" said a worried Rebecca Rabbit. "Oh, the more friends we have along, the more fun we'll have," replied the cheerful Sammy. "Don't worry. I packed plenty to eat!"

They were almost to the picnic rock when they passed Gunther Groundhog. Gunther saw the picnic basket and said, "Oh, I just love picnics. The day is perfect for the first Spring picnic. May I come along?" "Of course, please join us," replied the friendly squirrel. So Sammy Squirrel, Rebecca Rabbit, Roscoe Raccoon, Dorothy Deer, Benjamin Bear, and Gunther Groundhog continued on their journey until they reached picnic rock at last.

The animals were settling down on the picnic rock to enjoy their lunch when out of the water splashed Frederick Frog. Frederick saw the picnic basket and said, "Oh, I just love picnics . . ." Before Frederick could finish what he was going to say, Sammy and Rebecca began to laugh merrily. "Of course, please join us," replied the friendly squirrel. "The first picnic of the Spring has turned out to be a party for all our friends. We're happy to have you all with us!"

So Sammy Squirrel, Rebecca Rabbit, Roscoe Raccoon, Dorothy Deer, Benjamin Bear, Gunther Groundhog, and Frederick Frog all had a grand picnic at the picnic rock.

baby animal

picnic basket

baby animal

tree

130

Spring flowers—make 2

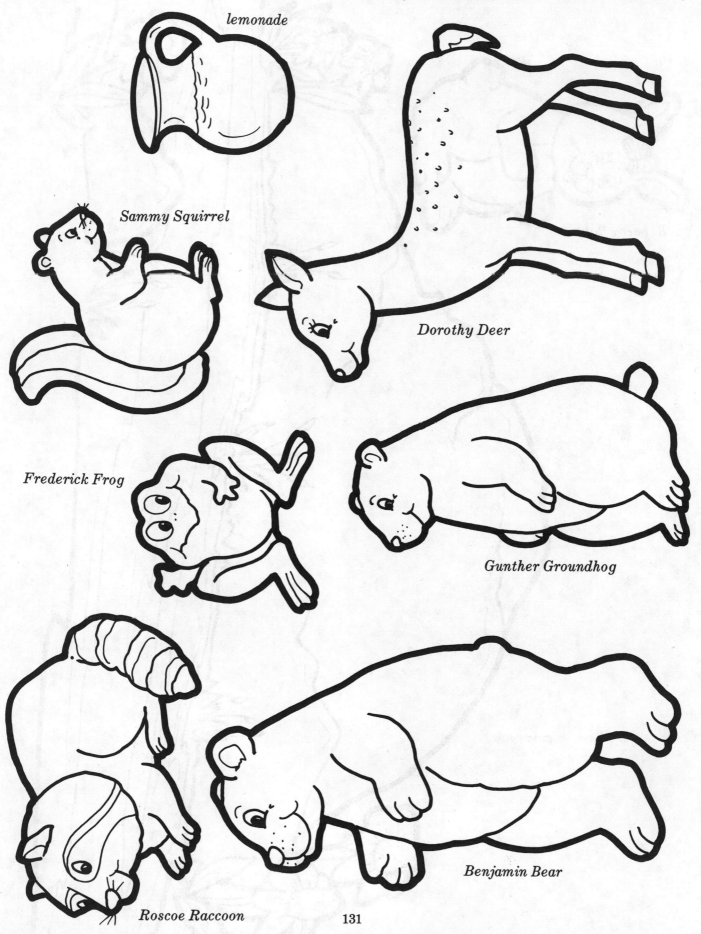

lemonade

Sammy Squirrel

Dorothy Deer

Frederick Frog

Gunther Groundhog

Roscoe Raccoon

Benjamin Bear

131

Rebecca Rabbit

picnic rock

Samantha the Story Mouse

One fine day in the Mountainview School*, Ms. Carole Roberts and the fifteen children in her class were sitting on the rug for story time. The children's names were Jay, Kim, Jerri, Steven, Melissa, Rodney, Becky, Andrew, Mary Beth, Tim, Gina, Brian, Laura, Keith and Kathryn. The children and their teacher loved story time, and as the children were getting settled on the rug, Ms. Roberts looked around the room and asked, "Children, do you see anything different in our story area today?"

Suddenly Jay said, "Look, there's a little house over by the corner of the rug."

"You're absolutely right," answered Ms. Roberts. "I saw it, too. Will you bring it over to me, please, Jay?"

Jay hurried to get the small house and brought it to his teacher.

Ms. Roberts held the house up for all the children to see. "What do you think this is?" she asked.

"It looks like a house for something very small," replied Jerri.

"Yes, the letters on the roof of the house say 'Samantha Story Mouse,'" said Ms. Roberts.

Suddenly there was a little squeak and the door to the house opened. Out hopped a small and surprised mouse. "Hello," she squeaked. "I am Samantha Story Mouse. And who are you?"

The children and Ms. Roberts introduced themselves to Samantha.

"Why are you called a story mouse?" asked Tim.

"Because my very favorite thing of all is to listen to stories. That's why I moved here. Someone told me that you have story time every day and I decided this would be a nice place to live. Do you mind if I join you?" Samantha asked.

"Oh, yes, please live with us!" the children answered.

"I do have one special request, though," said Samantha. "When I listen to stories, I like everyone to be very quiet so I can hear every word. Is that all right with you?"

"Oh, yes, we're very quiet when we listen to stories," the children replied. "Please stay with us and Ms. Roberts will tell us wonderful stories every day."

"Oh, thank you so much," said Samantha. "I know I'm going to be so happy here. I'll just settle down here by Ms. Roberts and we'll all listen to today's story together."

So Samantha Story Mouse found a new home and many new friends. Every day she came and quietly listened to the stories with the children.

*We suggest substituting the name of your school, your name, and the children's names to make the story more personal. Have your children introduce themselves to Samantha. Children love to hear about themselves as characters in the stories you tell, and they enjoy participating in the story telling!

Use the patterns on pages 134 to 135 to make this into a flannel board story, or make your own story mouse and house to discover in the corner of your room (see pages 136-137).

Samantha's house — cut door on dotted line;
fold back to find Samantha

Samantha #1

Samantha #2

"Samantha the Story Mouse" — Mouse and House

Materials:

1. Gray cotton fabric for body.
2. Gray felt for tail and ears.
3. Small black beads for eyes and nose.
4. Yarn for whiskers.
5. Fiberfill.
6. Container to make house out of.

Directions:

1. Cut pieces out: 2 of upper body and 1 of mouse bottom from gray cotton fabric, 2 of ear and 1 of tail from gray felt. (*Note:* seam allowances are not included in pattern.)
2. Sew upper body pieces together along longer curved edge; turn.
3. Sew bottom of mouse to upper body, leaving opening for turning at back of mouse. Turn; stuff with fiberfill. Insert tail. Stitch opening closed.
4. Fold ears at bottom, attach to body.
5. Make whiskers from yarn sewn to front of body (attach folded yarn to very front of body so all whiskers are attached at once instead of sewing half on each side).
6. Sew black beads to head for eyes and nose.
7. The house can be made from a recipe box, a shoe box, a cigar box, or any type of small container you have on hand.

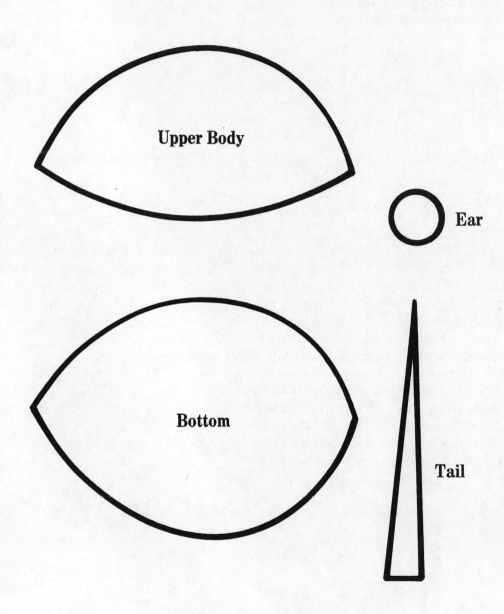

POCKET STORIES

The Fat Old Lady

Once there lived an old lady,
Who was extremely fat and wide;
She loved to snack on junk food,
And she never walked outside.

Every day she sat and watched TV,
And all she did was eat, eat, eat!

At one o'clock she ate a Big Mac;
At two o'clock she had some Cracker Jacks.

At three o'clock she ate a candy bar;
At four o'clock she had cookies from a jar.

At five o'clock she ate some french fries;
At six o'clock she had a lemon meringue pie.

At seven o'clock she ate some potato chips;
At eight o'clock she had a bag of peppermint sticks.

At nine o'clock she ate a hot dog on a bun;
At ten o'clock she had cotton candy just for fun.

At eleven o'clock she ate some chocolate cake;
At twelve o'clock she had a **stomachache!**

The Fat Old Lady—enlarge to poster board size; attach plastic bag behind hole for stomach and staple to poster board. Drop food in piece by piece while telling story.

Big Mac

Cracker Jacks

candy bar

cookies

french fries

peppermint sticks

143

cotton candy

lemon meringue pie

chocolate cake

CHIPS

potato chips

hot dog

144

Halloween Hilda

There once was a witch named Hilda,
Who loved Halloween night best of all.
She loved playing "flying broomstick,"
And with the goblins and ghosts had a ball.

But while the boys and girls were eating their treats,
Hilda grew so hungry that she heard her stomach call.
And then she ate through:

> 1 spider
> 2 bats
> 3 frogs
> 4 pumpkins, and
> 5 scary monsters!

Then Hilda's tummy was full of good witch's food,
And she went "whoosh" in the night on her broomstick,
Cackling and laughing in a fine Halloween mood!

Halloween Hilda—enlarge to poster board size; cover apron of skirt with a plastic bag or piece of plastic.

bat—make 2

frog—make 3

pumpkin—make 4

monster—make 5

spider

broomstick

Barnaby Bunny's Basket

There once was a bunny named Barnaby,
    Who lived on a hill so high.
Easter Day was his favorite time,
    And pretty Easter eggs he loved to dye.

Barnaby Bunny's basket held:
        1 blue egg
        2 green eggs
        3 yellow eggs
        4 pink eggs, and
        5 purple eggs

Then Barnaby delivered the Easter Baskets,
    As fast as his legs could fly.
And all the girls and boys thought Barnaby Bunny,
    Was really a very special guy!

Barnaby Bunny's Basket"—Pocket Story

Barnaby Bunny—enlarge to poster board size; cover basket with plastic.

egg—make 1 blue, 2 green, 3 yellow, 4 pink, 5 purple

Santa's Christmas Sack

Christmas Eve comes once each year,
And Santa has a job, I hear.
Santa Claus travels from far and near,
To deliver toys to you, my dears.

Santa's sack is full of toys,
Magic and marvelous and to enjoy;
For all the good little girls and boys,
To share in some special Christmas joy.

If into Santa's sack you should peek,
You will see the wonderful toys you seek:
A truck, a doll, and a mouse that squeaks,
A ball, a train, and a bear named Zeke.

A car, a book, and angels three,
A puzzle, a horn, and a dog named Lee.
This very Christmas Day, you'll see,
Toys from Santa's sack under your tree.

Santa's sack—enlarge to poster board size; cover sack with plastic.

doll

truck

mouse

ball

Zeke the bear

train

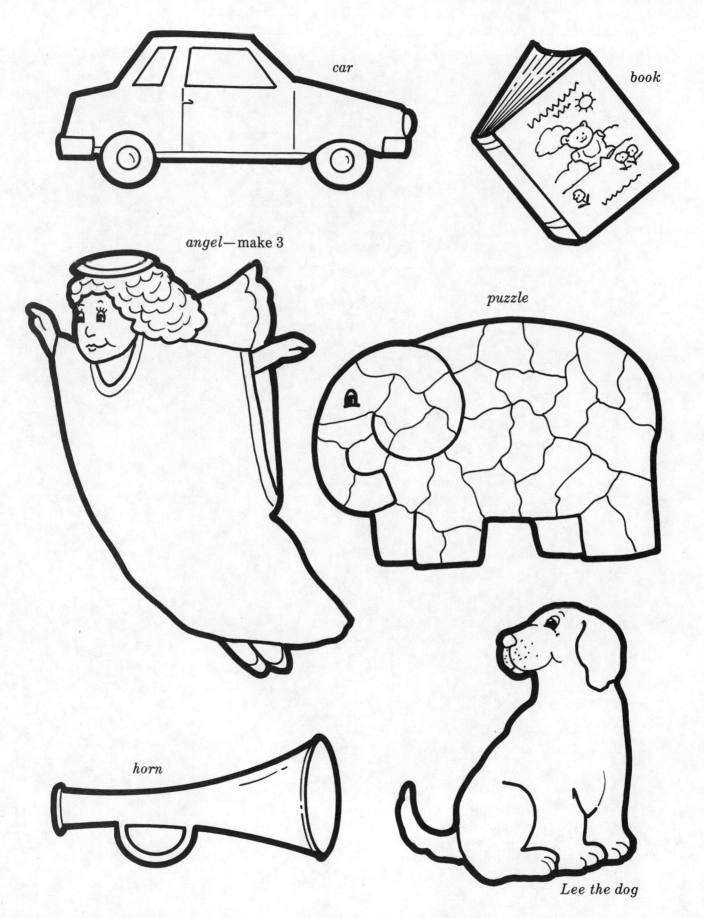

car

book

angel—make 3

puzzle

horn

Lee the dog

153

PUPPETS

Puppets provide a wonderful tool to use in story telling. They are especially appealing to children, because:

- They are moveable, life-like props that make stories come to life by involving many of the child's senses.
- They are appealing and nonthreatening, perhaps because they move and are rather funny-looking, perhaps because they are smaller than the child.
- They provide a mask for the shy child to hide behind while he or she is developing self-confidence.
- They offer a child the opportunity to work through emotional conflicts in a socially acceptable manner.
- They provide a method for acting out and coming to terms with real life experiences and roles.
- They provide unlimited possibilities for creativity, through puppet making, script writing, set and stage creation, and oral expression.
- They provide opportunities for language skills development through sequence, left-right progression, spatial relationships, oral expression, and listening skills.

Directions are included in this section for making puppets from a variety of materials. The children also enjoy being puppets themselves. They could write a short poem or song to accompany their puppet actions.

I am a puppet! Can you see,
The strings I have on me?

I can nod left, I can nod right,
I can even pretend to fight.

I can bend to touch my toes,
Or raise my finger to my nose.

I can lift a hand or lift a knee.
I really like the strings on me!

Hands and Feet Puppets

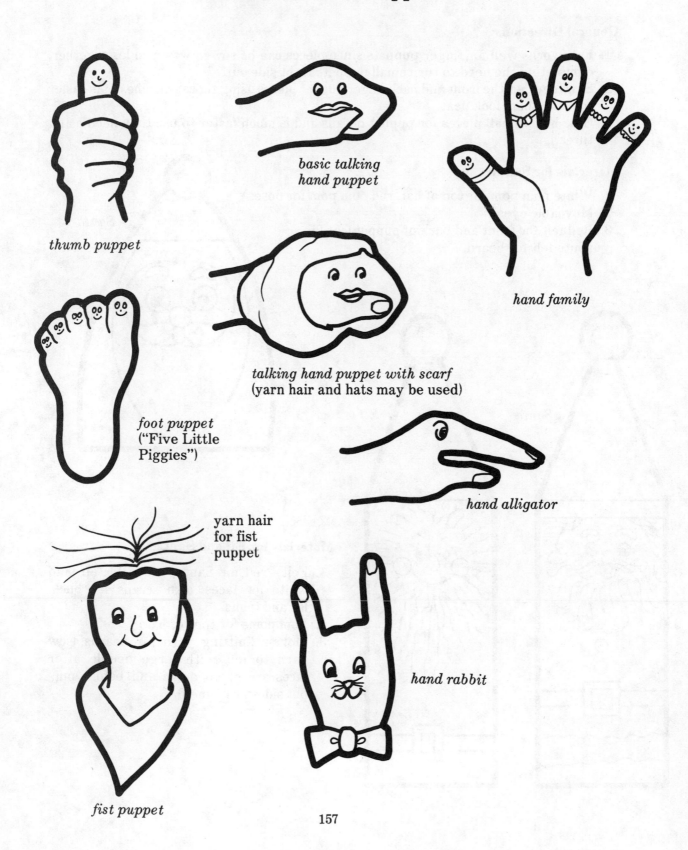

thumb puppet

basic talking
hand puppet

hand family

foot puppet
("Five Little
Piggies")

talking hand puppet with scarf
(yarn hair and hats may be used)

hand alligator

yarn hair
for fist
puppet

fist puppet

hand rabbit

Finger Puppets

General Directions:

1. Felt works well for finger puppets since pieces can be sewed wrong sides together, eliminating the need to turn small puppets right side out.
2. Sew together the front and back finger puppet pieces using zig-zag stitches. It is easier to make them look neat.
3. Glue holds small pieces for puppet details and is much faster to use than needle and thread.

Materials for Santa:

1. White pom pom for top of hat, red pom pom for nose.
2. Moveable eyes.
3. Red felt for front and back of puppet (cut 2), white felt for beard.

Santa

Santa   *Elf*

Materials for Elf and Santa:

1. Felt—red for Santa, green for elf, and white for faces; also scraps for buckles and trims.
2. Pom poms for tops of hats.
3. Mohair knitting yarn for beards (sew yarn to felt with large needle after faces are glued down and before puppet sides are joined).

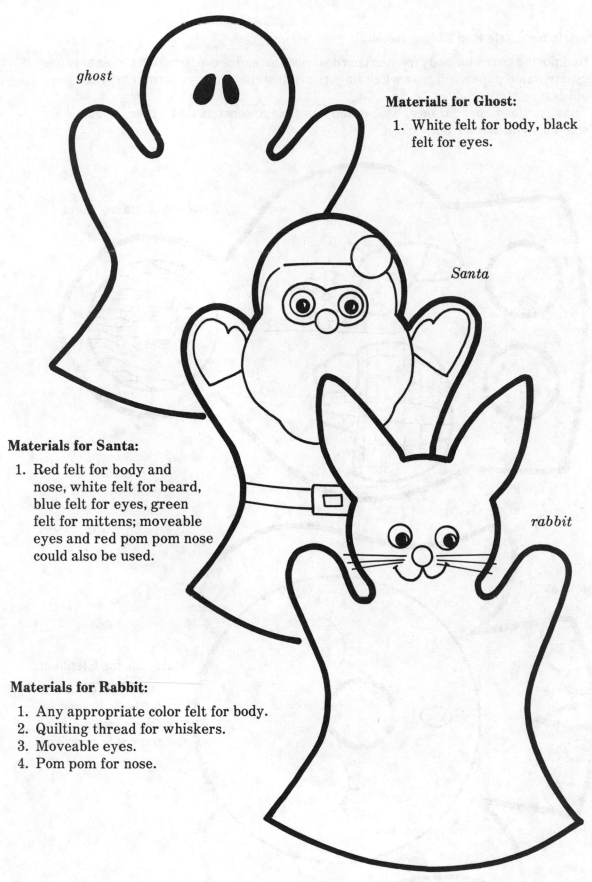

ghost

Materials for Ghost:

1. White felt for body, black felt for eyes.

Santa

Materials for Santa:

1. Red felt for body and nose, white felt for beard, blue felt for eyes, green felt for mittens; moveable eyes and red pom pom nose could also be used.

rabbit

Materials for Rabbit:

1. Any appropriate color felt for body.
2. Quilting thread for whiskers.
3. Moveable eyes.
4. Pom pom for nose.

Materials for Little Red Riding Hood:

1. Red poster board for body (poster board is used instead of construction paper because construction paper will tear when fingers are inserted; fingers form legs when puppet is operated).
2. Construction paper for face, basket and hair (fringe construction paper for hair; hair could also be made from yarn).

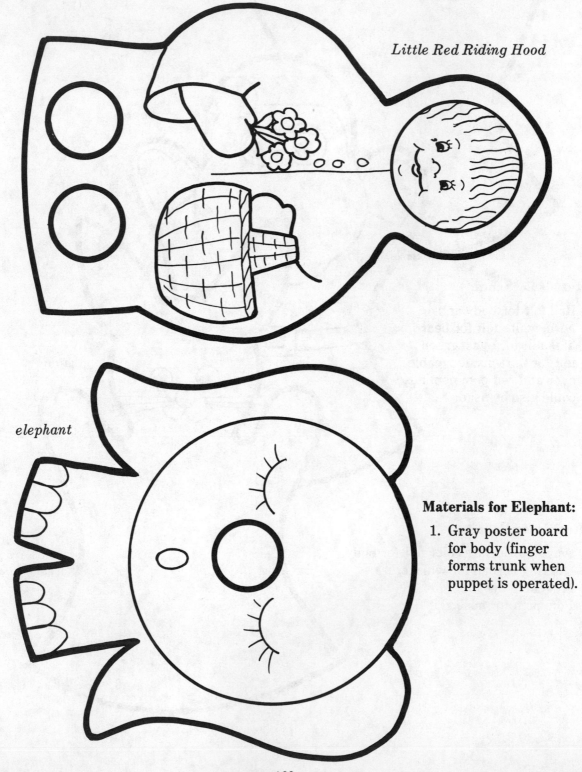

Little Red Riding Hood

elephant

Materials for Elephant:

1. Gray poster board for body (finger forms trunk when puppet is operated).

160

Paper Bag Puppets

paper bag owl— feathers are made from small pieces of construction paper

paper bag Santa

paper bag puppet with stuffed head— hair is made from curled construction paper

lengthwise bag puppet

rabbit puppet— use a large grocery bag for the rabbit; cut a circle for the child's face

whole body puppet— the child's head shows above this puppet; paper plate can be used for the head with a large grocery bag forming the body; legs and arms can be made of fabric or paper; strings are used to attach puppet to child

Paper Plate Puppets

Puppets can be made from any size or shape of paper plate, including divided plates (rabbit on next page is made from 3-sectioned plate). Plates may be made into puppets by:

• Adding a stick to the bottom of the plate.
• Adding half of another plate to the back of the plate.
• Cutting one plate in half and attaching it to a folded plate (mouth puppet).
• Joining other parts to the plate to make a whole body puppet.

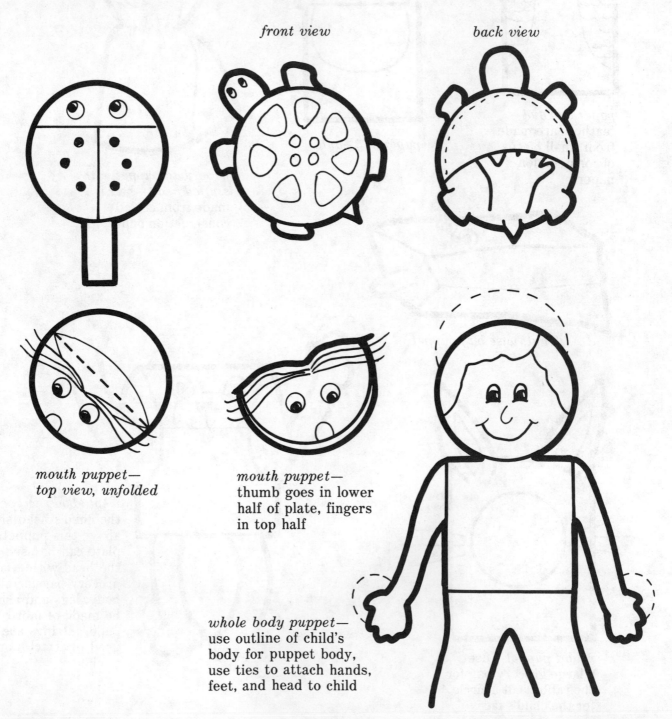

front view

back view

*mouth puppet—
top view, unfolded*

*mouth puppet—
thumb goes in lower
half of plate, fingers
in top half*

*whole body puppet—
use outline of child's
body for puppet body,
use ties to attach hands,
feet, and head to child*

fire fighter

police officer

baker

doctor

nurse

mail carrier

"self" puppet—
(cut out eyes)

pumpkin puppet

turkey puppet—
construction paper
loops make feathers

Santa

rabbit—3-section
plate, small sections
form cheeks

Easter basket—2
plates stapled on
sides with portion
cut out for handle

Paper Cup Puppets

Paper, styrofoam, and plastic disposable cups provide inexpensive bases for puppets that result in successful products, even with very young children. A more durable puppet can be made from empty ready-to-spread frosting containers. Adhesive papers with pull-off backings will stick to styrofoam and plastic cups. Colored circles can be purchased at office supply stores and used for eyes and noses. Unused name tags can be cut into mouth shapes.

figure—styrofoam ball for head, chenille strips form arms and legs

boy—hair is attached by putting it through small hole in cup

paper cup with finger nose

turtle—shell is made from top third of a styrofoam cup

giraffe

animal—to make workable mouth, cut cup and tape a folded insert to form middle of mouth

Christmas tree

Cups can be used to make pop-up puppets, also.

pop-up flower—for spring science lessons

clown—head is styrofoam ball; glue stick to ball

bird and nest—make bird from circles or pom poms; nest is ⅓ cup wrapped with construction paper strips

pop-up squirrel—decorate cup to look like a tree for squirrel's home

Envelope Puppets

Envelope puppets can be made from regular or legal-sized envelopes, or by constructing an envelope from paper.

Envelope Puppet, Version 1:

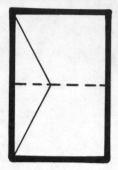

fold envelope in half

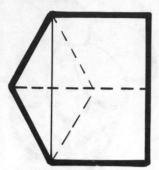

unfold and cut on folded line through back of envelope only

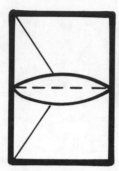

seal flap of envelope

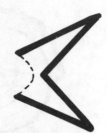

fold in half again; insert fingers in top of envelope, thumb in bottom of envelope

Envelope Puppet, Version 2 (made from construction paper):

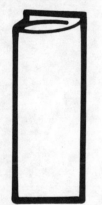

fold 8½″ x 11″ piece of construction paper into thirds, lengthwise

fold in half

fold into fourths; insert fingers into top, thumb into bottom of paper

alligator—made from legal-sized envelope or larger construction paper, tape teeth to envelope

fox

pig

dog

rabbit (pom pom nose)

frog (curled tongue)

166

Envelope Puppet, Version 3:

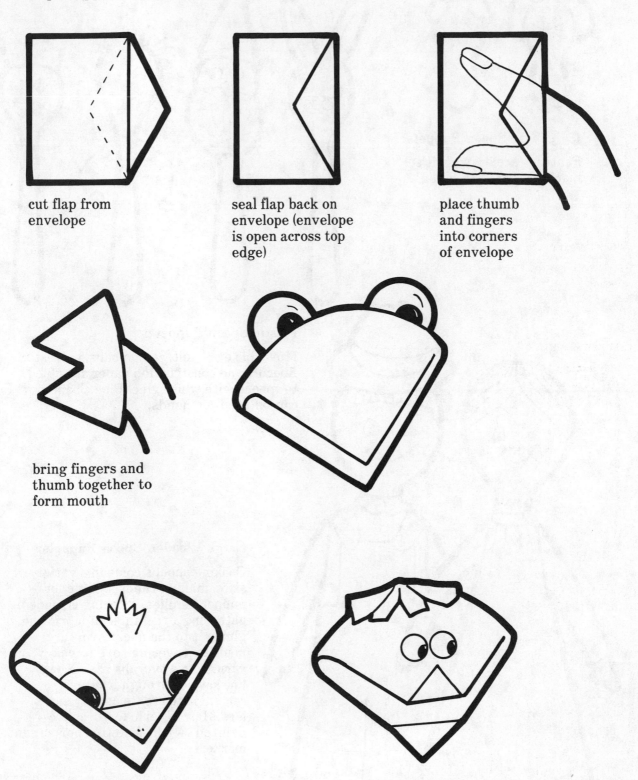

cut flap from
envelope

seal flap back on
envelope (envelope
is open across top
edge)

place thumb
and fingers
into corners
of envelope

bring fingers and
thumb together to
form mouth

Legal-sized envelopes can also be used for this type of puppet.

Spoon Puppets

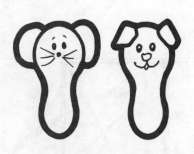

Ice Cream Spoon Puppets:

Features are drawn with markers; ears are glued.

Plastic Spoon Puppets:

Moveable eyes, felt, cotton balls, polyester fiberfill, and construction paper are glued to spoons with white glue. Pipe cleaners can be used for hands.

Large Wooden Spoon Puppets:

Cooking spoons come in a variety of sizes, making them suitable for puppet families. Clothing is made by gathering a rectangle of fabric and gluing it to the neck. Arms are made by covering rope or heavy yarn. Man's overalls have a heavy line sewed through front of rectangle to create appearance of legs. Hair is yarn; features are painted with fine-tip permanent markers.

dog—spoon is painted brown to match brown felt used for body and ears; glue-on eyes were used; pom poms make nose, cheeks and paws; mouth was made from red felt; large circle on body was cut from white felt

witch—dress and hat are made of black cotton fabric; features are drawn with black marker; hair is "pre-crinkled" by winding around a small piece of poster board and ironing before gluing to spoon; broom may be made or purchased

baby—dress made from 6" pre-gathered eyelet trim

boy—made from wooden spatula; shoes are felt

Stick Puppets

Toothpicks, popsicle sticks, tongue depressors, straws, dowel rods, and broom handles can all be turned into puppets.

Small Stick Puppets (toothpicks, popsicle sticks, tongue depressors):

snowman—glue pom poms to a stick

bear—commercial sticker attached to a tongue depressor

pumpkin—cut from felt

doll—cut from discarded greeting card (catalog pictures may also be used, especially if backed with firm paper)

Santa—plastic cake decoration; break off plastic toothpick part and glue to tongue depressor if you need a longer handle

marshmallow snowman—dip toothpicks in food coloring to make facial features

owl—embroidered fabric appliques make colorful puppets

Larger Stick Puppets (dowel rods and broom handles):

snowman—made from styrofoam balls and dowel rod; carefully punch dowel into balls, remove dowel, add glue, return dowel; to give snowman a more realistic look, slightly flatten balls where they meet by pressing against table

girl—made from styrofoam ball, styrofoam cone, and dowel rod; follow same gluing procedure as used for snowman; commercial thread cone may be used in place of styrofoam cone

hobo—made from styrofoam ball and cardboard box (glue box to bottom of head to prevent sliding); beard is fake fur, glued on; hat was purchased at craft store; chenille strips form arms

dancing man (based on traditional Appalachian toy)—body is cut from ½″ wood with hole drilled ¼″ into back; dowel is glued into this hole; arms and legs are dowel rods with small holes drilled at each joint; insert thread through each hole and join by making a thread loop

moveable eyes and
a pom pom nose are
added to a dish mop

empty detergent
bottle fits onto
a dowel rod

child-size broom covered from
the handle end with the toe of a
sock; features are applied to the
sock; broom forms the hair

toothpick hair and cut
features are added to
potato and apple puppets

elephant—fold half of a
9″ x 12″ piece of
gray construction
paper into thirds;
cut as shown on dotted
lines; (dotted lines
on puppet illustration
are fold lines)

broom stick puppets using commercial ice cream
container or gallon milk jug make very large
puppets; nail through the top of the container
into the top of the broomstick if you do not want
the puppet to wobble; omit nail if you like the
wobble

Box Puppets

tin man—made from boxes painted gray or covered with foil; join boxes by punching two holes in each box and tying circle of thread between them; note string connecting feet designed to give "Soldier" walk, normally string would go to knee

girl—made from box, styrofoam ball, and macrame cord; hands may be made from beads or by making knots in the cord; knots may also be used to make knees and elbows

snake—made of joined boxes; this puppet is easy for a very young child to operate

mouth puppet—made by cutting a box in half on three sides, or by taping two boxes together

stick and hand puppets may also be made from boxes

Sock Puppets

cut mouth from toe inward

insert folded material for mouth

mark and cut material for mouth

sew mouth into sock

hand puppet—a tube sock stuffed with a styrofoam ball

snake—tube sock with tongue sewn in

caterpillar—tube sock stuffed with styrofoam balls; tie between each ball; close end of sock

Mitt Puppets

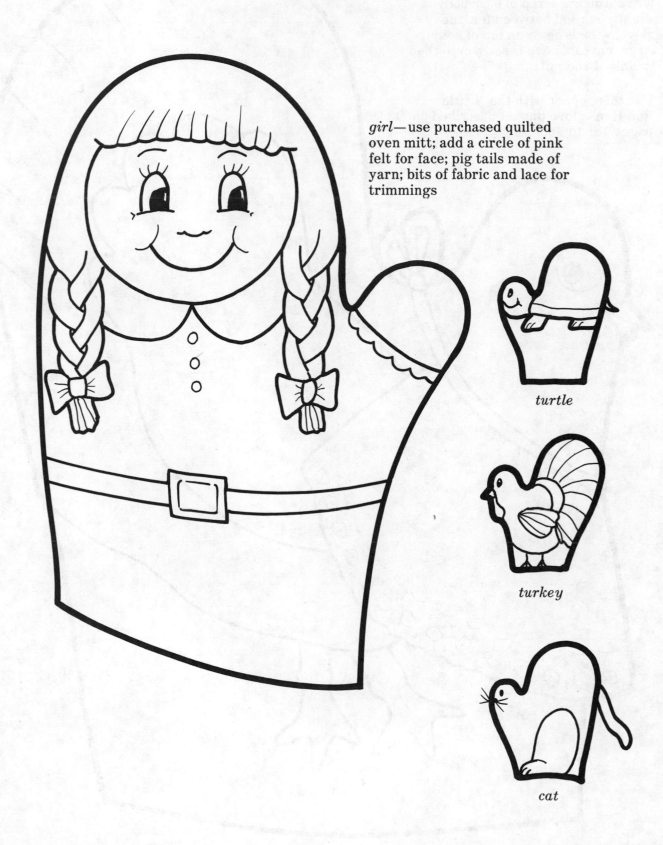

girl—use purchased quilted oven mitt; add a circle of pink felt for face; pig tails made of yarn; bits of fabric and lace for trimmings

turtle

turkey

cat

"Little Red Hen" *mitt puppet*—red felt body stitched to an oven mitt; legs and beak are made of yellow felt; apron is a scrap of lace; body is slightly stuffed between felt and glove; wing is sewn on top of body; large moveable eye is sewn onto the thumb of the mitt

Use this puppet with the "Little Red Hen" glove puppet described on pages 181 to 182.

Glove Puppets

This section includes directions for making pom pom glove puppets and soft sculptured glove puppets. If a simpler glove puppet is desired, adapt these ideas and use felt and glue to create the puppet characters.

Pom Pom Glove Puppets

General Directions:

1. Use work gloves that do not have a definite right and left hand. (The thumb will stick out equally to the side of the glove when viewed from front or back.) This allows both gloves in the pair to be used for puppets; the characters will stand up in a row without the thumb character being beneath the first finger character. The center of the glove should be free for decoration. Color selection depends on the use of the glove. If characters are detailed and viewing will be at close range, use a dark glove that will not distract from the characters. If characters are simple and viewing will be from several feet, use a white or brightly colored glove to attract attention.

2. Faces for puppet characters can be created using pom poms, felt, and beads. To create a face for a bearded man, cut a small oblong piece of flesh-colored felt. Fold the felt in half crosswise and sew very close to the fold to create a nose. Open the felt and sew on small black beads for eyes (or glue on moveable eyes). Trim the pom pom slightly in the area the face will be placed. Glue on the face, then glue trimmings of pom pom around the edges of felt so edges are hidden. If you sew the pom pom on the glove before gluing on the face, the knot can be hidden beneath the felt.

   To create a face for a person without a beard, cut face from felt and sew nose halfway down felt. Add eyes and glue face to trimmed area of pom pom. Be sure felt reaches bottom of pom pom so no "hair" shows beneath the face. Glue trimmings on top and sides, but not bottom of face.

   Animals can be made by combining different sizes of pom poms or adding felt snouts, noses and ears.

bearded   *non-bearded*

3. Thread, glue and iron-on adhesives ("Stitch Witchery") can be used to assemble the puppet. If the puppet will be used frequently, sew and glue the pom poms in place. The middle of the glove may be sewn, bonded, or glued.

4. The glove should be constructed so the characters are on the palm side. When telling the story, first fold down fingers (make a fist) and then lift each finger as that character is introduced to the story.

"The Three Pigs"—Pom Pom Glove Puppet

Materials:

1. Three 1½″ pink pom poms and three smaller pink pom poms for pigs, one gray 1½″ pom pom for wolf.
2. Felt: pink, gray, various colors for pigs' clothing, stick and brick houses.
3. Small black beads for pigs' eyes and wolf's eyes and nose. (Moveable eyes could be used for the pigs' eyes, also).
4. Various colors of embroidery thread.

"The Three Pigs"—Glove Puppet

Directions:

1. Pigs are made from 1½″ pom poms with a small pom pom for the nose. Trim the sides of the small pom pom so it looks like a cylinder instead of a circle. Slightly trim the large pom pom where the nose will be placed. Cut triangles of pink felt for ears. Fold down top of triangle. Glue or sew ears in place. Eyes are small black beads. Clothing is made from felt. Use different colored overalls for each pig.
2. Wolf is made from light gray 1½″ pom pom. Add gray felt face, nose and ears. Eyes and end of nose are small black beads.
3. Straw house is embroidered. Stick and brick houses are felt applique.

Soft Sculpture Glove Puppets

General Directions:

1. Use dark hose because colors lighten when fiberfill is added. Several layers of hose may be used.
2. Begin with circles or oblongs. Gather with needle and thread around outer edge of circle. (Machine stitching causes runs.) Stuff lightly for flat heads; firmly for round heads.
3. If noses are small, create by stuffing small portions of circle used for head **before** stuffing rest of head. If noses are large, make a separate circle and sew to head.
4. Sew features from back of head circle after stuffing head. Pull thread firmly to flatten features into face. Make ears by pulling out and stitching small portions of head.
5. Don't be afraid to experiment. Use your creativity.

"The Three Bears" — Soft Sculpture Glove Puppet

Materials:

1. Dark brown nylon hose for bears' faces; flesh-colored hose for Goldilocks.
2. Polyester fiberfill.
3. Pom poms for noses: two ¼″ dark brown ones for Papa and Mama Bear, smaller brown one for Baby Bear.
4. Embroidery thread for details on characters and for house.
5. Various colors of felt for clothing for characters and for house.
6. Beads for eyes.
7. Yellow baby yarn for Goldilocks' hair.

"The Three Bears"—Glove Puppet

Directions:

• *Papa and Mama Bear*

1. Cut a 2½″ circle from dark brown nylon hose for Papa Bear's head and a 1¼″ circle for his nose. Mama Bear needs a 2″ circle for her head and a 1″ circle for her nose. (Circle sizes may vary according to the amount of stretch in the hose and the amount of stuffing used.)

2. Sew a row of gathering stitches around the outside of each circle with a double strand of thread. Leave needles attached.

3. Stuff large circles slightly with polyester fiberfill. Stuffing too firmly will cause the head to be too lightly colored and too round to fit against the glove. Pull up gathering thread, but do not cut thread.

4. Gather and stuff small circles for noses. Knot and cut the thread on these. Sew on small pom poms for tips of noses. Sew loop shapes beneath nose with black thread: make two large loops and tack at the bottom (see illustration on page 179).

5. Using thread attached to large circle, sew through back of head into side of nose. Blindstitch nose to head from back of head so nose is slightly flattened to head. Knot and cut thread after attaching nose.

6. Make ears by pinching up a portion of head and sewing with two large "V"-shaped stitches (\/). Sew black beads for eyes from back of head circle so they flatten into head.

7. Make hats and clothing from felt and sew to glove. (Hats may also be purchased at craft stores or sometimes found on hair barrettes.)

• *Baby Bear*

1. Baby Bear's face is made from a 1½″ circle. Directions are the same as Papa and Mama Bears', except that nose is created by stuffing a small portion of the head circle and wrapping it with thread rather than adding another circle.

Stuff nose, wrap thread, push needle to back of nose, knot and cut thread. Stuff remainder of head. After completing head circle, sew on pom pom nose and pull tightly to flatten nose circle against head circle.

• *Goldilocks*

1. Use 2″ circle of hose. Create nose by pulling out very small stuffed circle from front of 2″ circle (same as Baby Bear, only smaller circle). Stuffed nose should be about a ¼″ circle. Mouth is made with two stitches of double red thread pulled tightly against the face (see illustration on page 179). Use beads for eyes. Make hair from yellow baby yarn.

"The Little Red Hen" — Soft Sculpture Glove Puppet

Materials:

1. Nylon hose: gray for mouse, brown for cow, green for frog, black for cat, pink for pig.
2. Felt: gray for mouse, black for mouse, brown for cow, green for frog, red for cow, beaks of birds and barn, colors as desired for birds' hats.
3. Assorted colors of embroidery thread.
4. Beads for eyes and noses.
5. Moveable eyes for Little Red Hen's chicks.
6. Covered wires for cat's whiskers.
7. Yellow pom poms for Little Red Hen's chicks.

*Front of Glove Puppet
for "The Little Red Hen"*

Directions:

1. Put mouse, cow, frog, cat, pig and barn on the front side of the glove.
2. Mouse head is soft sculpture, made using gray nylon hose. Add large gray felt ears and tail, and a small black felt nose. Black thread forms line beneath nose; beads form eyes.
3. Cow is soft sculpture using brown hose. Nose is a separate soft sculpture oval attached to face; ears are pinched and sewn from head. Cow has felt ears, tongue, and nostrils; eyes are beads.

4. Frog has green soft sculpture body. Eye circles are pinched and sewn from head. Arms and legs are felt, black thread forms mouth, eye balls are beads.

5. Cat has soft sculpture head, with separate circle for nose. Ears are pinched and sewn from head. Red thread forms line beneath nose; nose and eyes are beads; whiskers are covered wires.

6. Pig has soft sculpture head, with separate circle for nose. Nostrils are sewn with pink thread pulled tightly; ears and chin are formed by pinching and sewing head. Eyes are beads.

7. Barn is constructed of felt. Yellow wheat growing next to barn is embroidered.

8. Put the Little Red Hen's chicks, and a fence and trees on the back side of the glove.

9. Chicks are made from yellow pom poms. Beaks are red felt and moveable eyes are glued on. Felt and pom pom hats may be used.

10. Make fence and trees using felt applique and embroidery.

11. Use this glove puppet with the "Little Red Hen" mitt puppet, described on page 176.

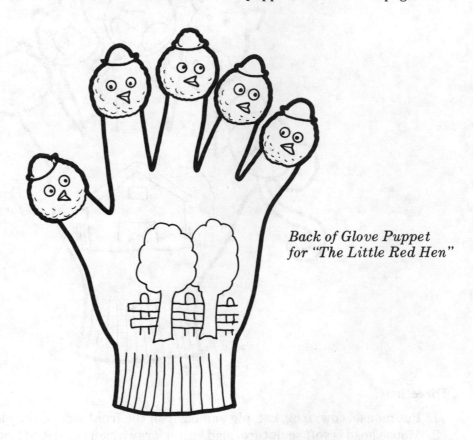

*Back of Glove Puppet
for "The Little Red Hen"*

Hand Puppets

This basic felt hand puppet pattern can be used in many ways. The use of felt allows you to sew the front and back pieces wrong sides together, eliminating the need to turn the puppet right side out.

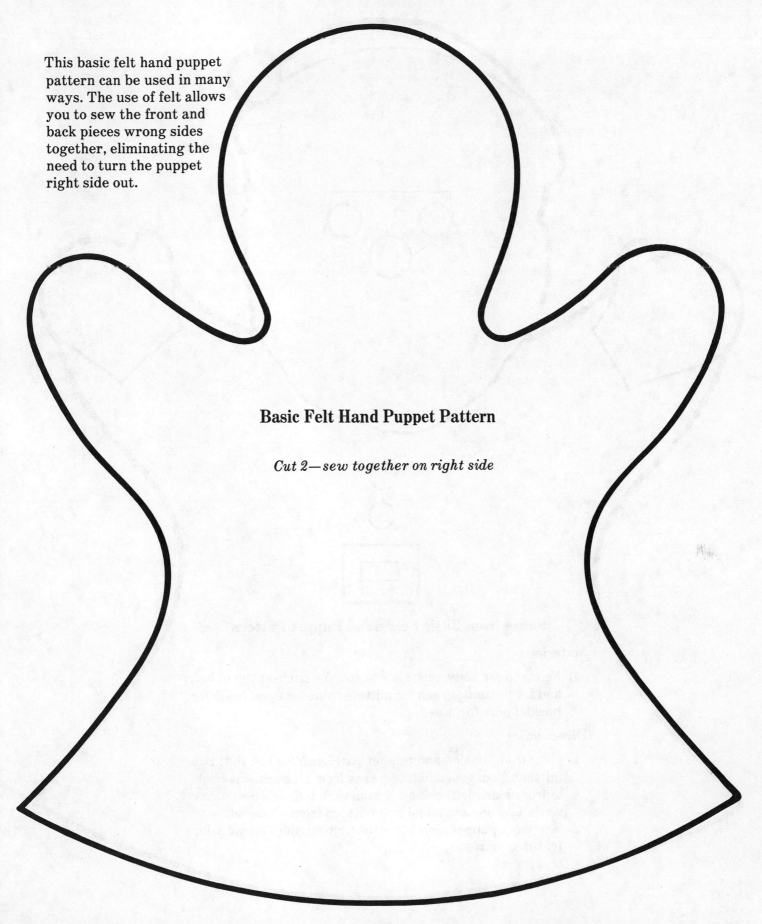

Basic Felt Hand Puppet Pattern

Cut 2—sew together on right side

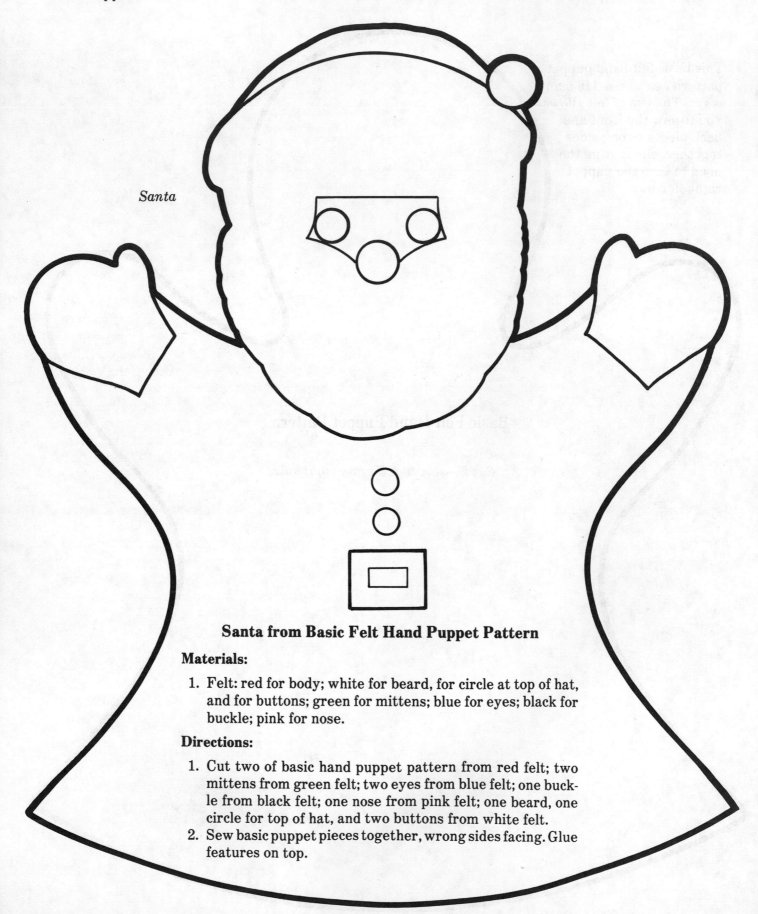

Santa

Santa from Basic Felt Hand Puppet Pattern

Materials:

1. Felt: red for body; white for beard, for circle at top of hat, and for buttons; green for mittens; blue for eyes; black for buckle; pink for nose.

Directions:

1. Cut two of basic hand puppet pattern from red felt; two mittens from green felt; two eyes from blue felt; one buckle from black felt; one nose from pink felt; one beard, one circle for top of hat, and two buttons from white felt.
2. Sew basic puppet pieces together, wrong sides facing. Glue features on top.

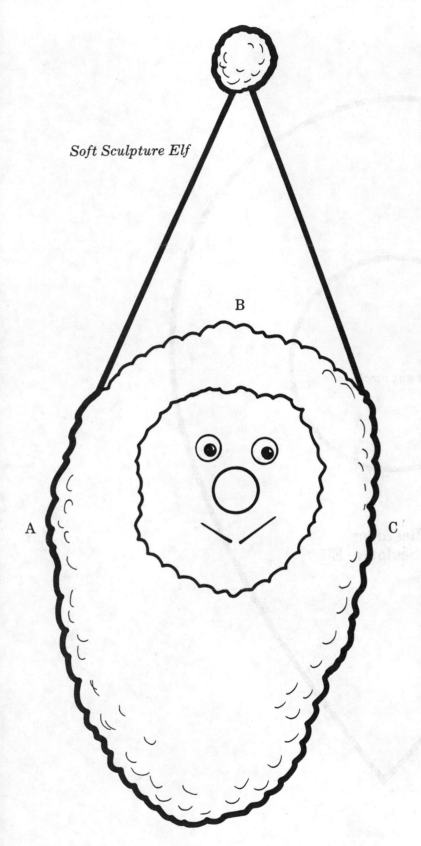

Soft Sculpture Elf

Soft Sculpture Elf from Basic Felt Hand Puppet Pattern

Materials:

1. Green or red felt for body.
2. Nylon hose.
3. Fiberfill.
4. Pom pom for top of hat.
5. ¼″ black beads or sew-on moveable eyes.
6. White fur for beard.
7. Red embroidery thread for mouth.

Directions:

1. Alter head on basic felt hand puppet pattern so it has a pointed hat (cut pointed paper pattern and tape to basic pattern before cutting felt).
2. Cut two of basic pattern from red or green felt.
3. Sew around edges of puppet, wrong sides together.
4. Make soft sculpture head. Cut 4½″ circle of nylon hose; gather around edge; stuff with fiberfill; pull gathering thread tight and knot thread.
5. To make nose, cut 1″ circle of hose, gather; stuff; knot thread.
6. Sew nose to face, pulling thread until face is almost flat where nose is attached.
7. Sew on eyes, pulling tight to flatten face.
8. Make mouth by taking two large stitches with red thread.
9. Cut one of beard pattern (see page 186) from white long-haired fur. Cut fur from wrong side, cutting through backing only. Sew right side of inner circle of beard to outer edge of face, turning under edge to prevent raw edge from showing.
10. Sew outer edge of beard to puppet body from bottom of face (point A, see illustration at left), across top of face (to point B), and back to other side (point C). Turn under raw edge while sewing. Leave bottom of beard free.

185

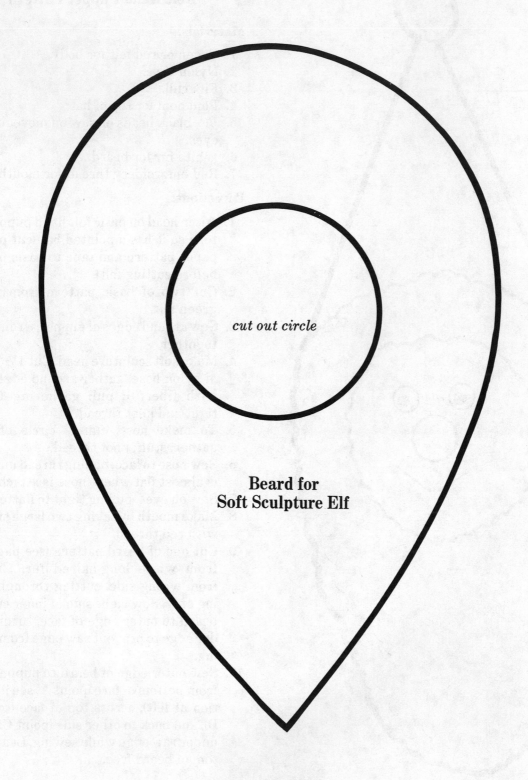

cut out circle

**Beard for
Soft Sculpture Elf**

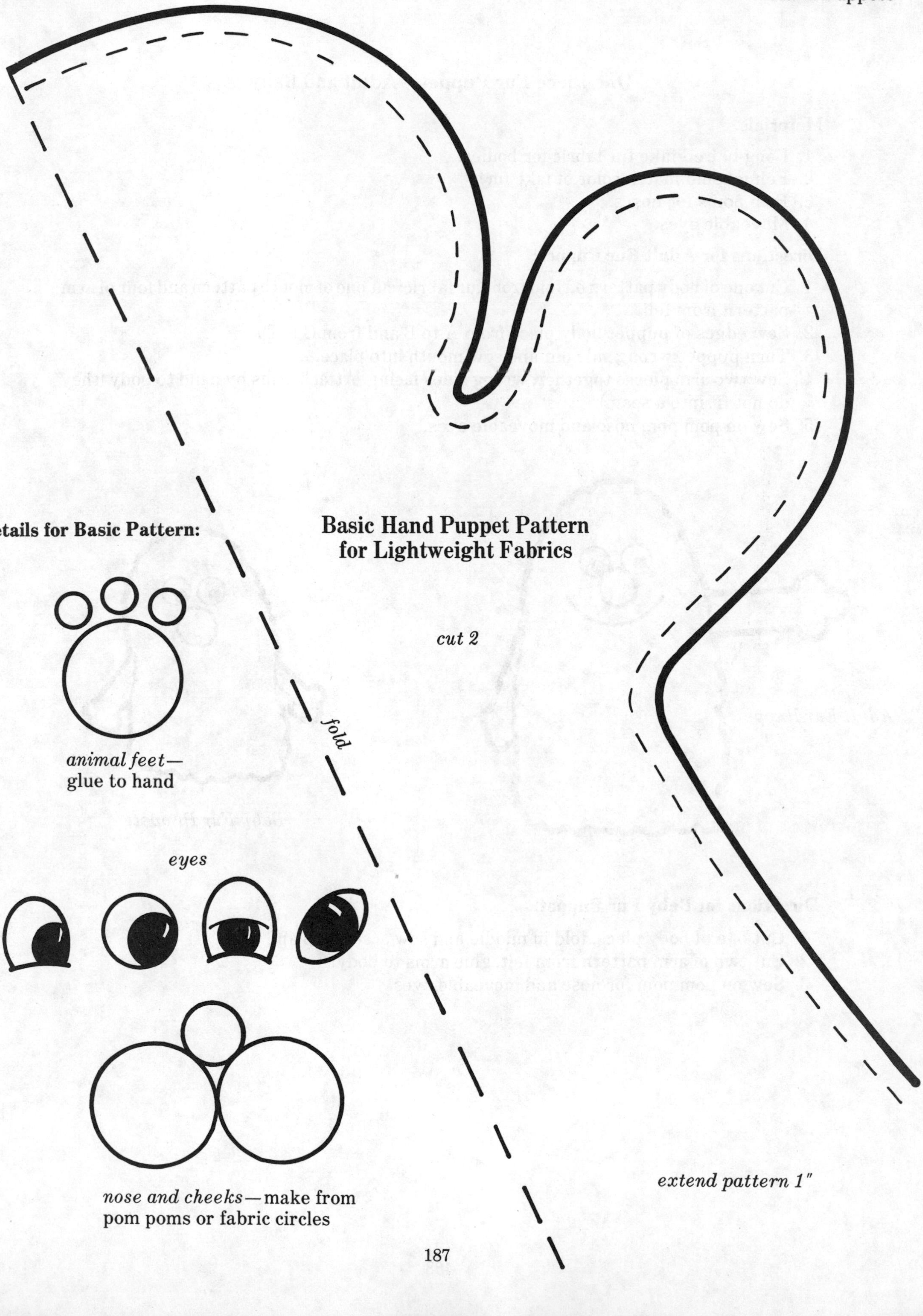

Details for Basic Pattern:

**Basic Hand Puppet Pattern
for Lightweight Fabrics**

cut 2

fold

*animal feet—
glue to hand*

eyes

nose and cheeks—make from
pom poms or fabric circles

extend pattern 1"

187

One-Piece Fur Puppet—Adult and Baby

Materials:

1. Long-haired fake fur fabric for bodies.
2. Felt (should match color of fake fur).
3. Pom poms for noses.
4. Moveable eyes.

Directions for Adult Fur Puppet:

1. Cut one of body pattern on fold from fur fabric; cut one of mouth pattern and four of arm pattern from felt.
2. Sew edges of puppet body piece from A to B and from C to D.
3. Turn puppet wrong side out and sew mouth into place.
4. Sew two arm pieces together, wrong sides facing. Attach arms by hand to body (they do not fit into a seam).
5. Sew on pom pom nose and moveable eyes.

Adult Fur Puppet

Baby Fur Puppet

Directions for Baby Fur Puppet:

1. Cut one of body piece, fold in middle and sew across top and side.
2. Cut two of arm pattern from felt, glue arms to body.
3. Sew on pom pom for nose and moveable eyes.

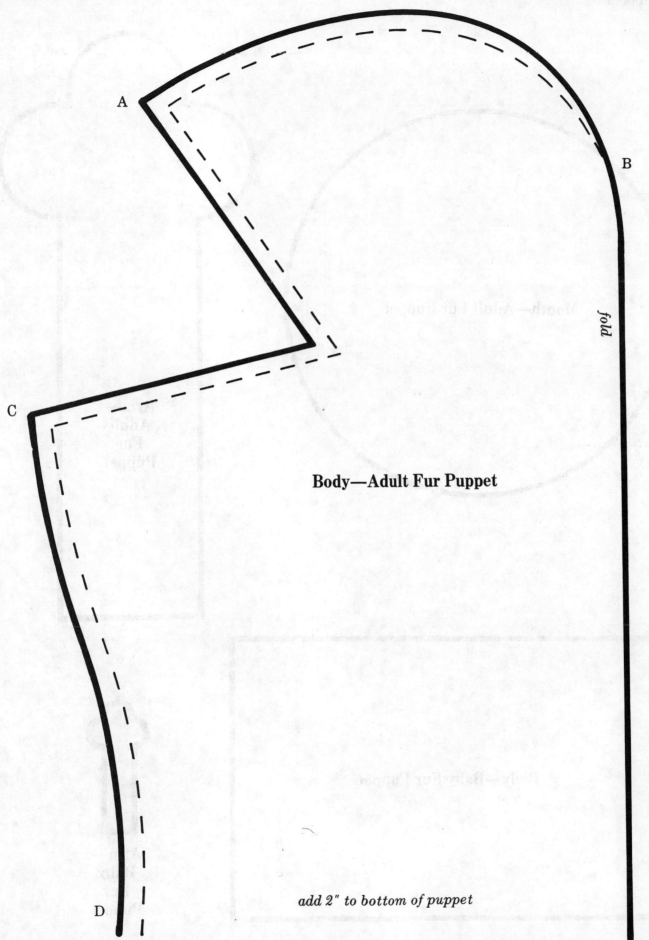

A

B

fold

Body—Adult Fur Puppet

C

D

add 2" to bottom of puppet

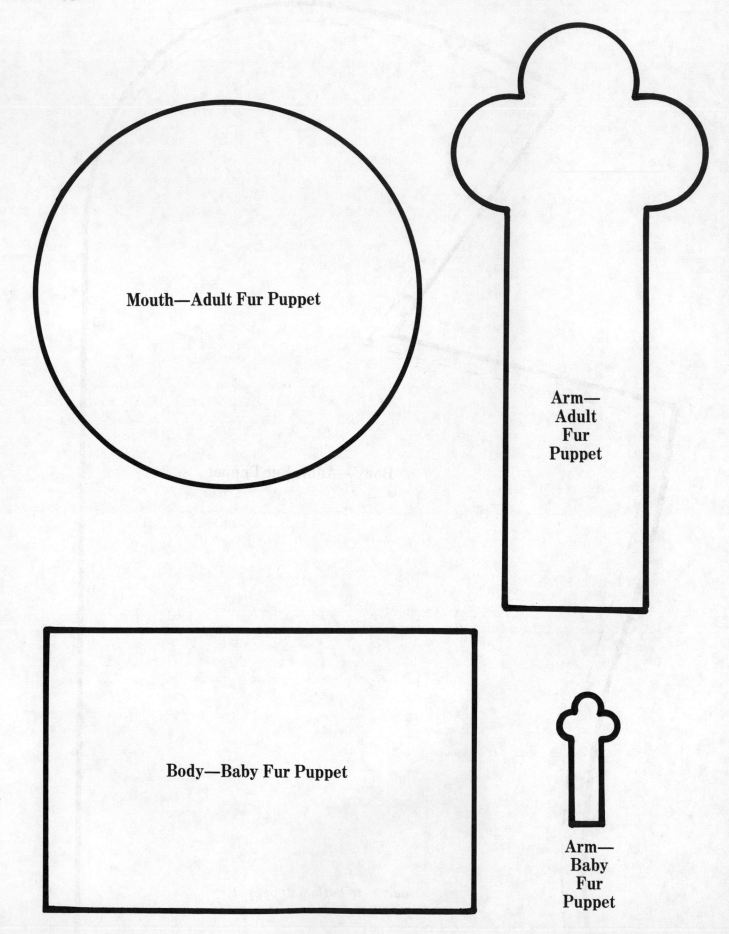

Mouth—Adult Fur Puppet

Arm—
Adult
Fur
Puppet

Body—Baby Fur Puppet

Arm—
Baby
Fur
Puppet

Skunk Hand Puppet

Materials:

1. Fake fur: black and white.
2. White felt to line ears.
3. Black pom pom for nose.
4. Moveable eyes.

Skunk Hand Puppet

Directions:

1. When cutting fake fur, lay pattern on back side of fur, mark with chalk, and then cut through fabric backing only. Do not cut the fur itself.
2. Cut two of pattern piece A from black fake fur. Cut one of pattern piece B from black fur. (For pattern piece B, construct complete paper pattern before cutting. Do not try to cut fur on the fold.) Join pattern pieces D1 and D2 along dotted lines before cutting; cut one of white fur. Join pattern pieces E1 and E2 on dotted lines before cutting; cut one of black fur. Cut 2 of pattern piece C from black fur and 2 of piece C from white felt.
3. Cut pattern piece D (white stripe) along dashed line (see pattern). Insert black stripe into slashed area. (Use ¼ " seams in constructing the skunk.) Sew on both sides so a long piece of white fur with a black stripe down the center is formed.
4. Attach pattern piece A (sides of skunk body) to pattern piece B (bottom of skunk body). The pointed end of the bottom piece goes toward the front and ends where the pointed end of the tail piece will begin. Leave open between X marks (hand goes in beneath tail to operate puppet).
5. Begin sewing tail piece (white and black stripe) in where point from bottom of skunk ends. After sewing both sides of stripe to sides of body, fold remaining part of tail piece, forming top and bottom for tail. Sew tail, rounding corners.
6. Narrow-hem seam allowance around opening for hand. Tack down underside of tail.
7. Make ears (pattern piece C) by sewing one felt ear and one fur ear together, right sides facing. Turn ears, fold bottom of each together and tack into place on skunk.
8. Sew on pom pom nose and moveable eyes.

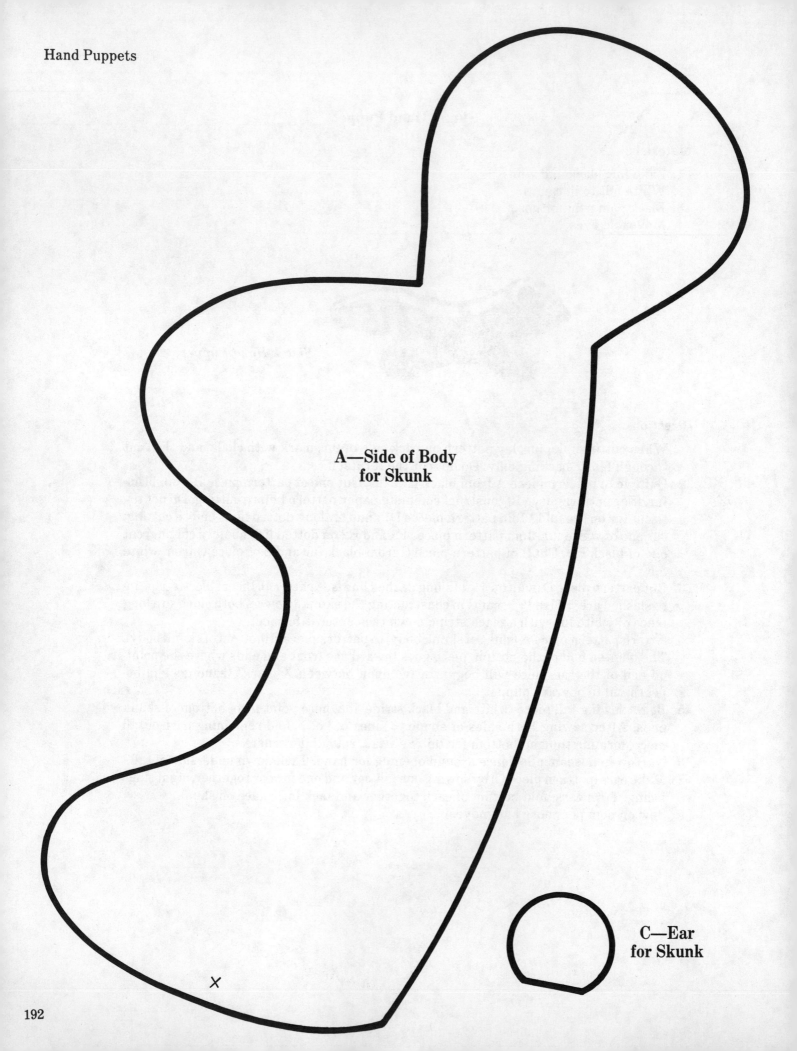

A—Side of Body
for Skunk

C—Ear
for Skunk

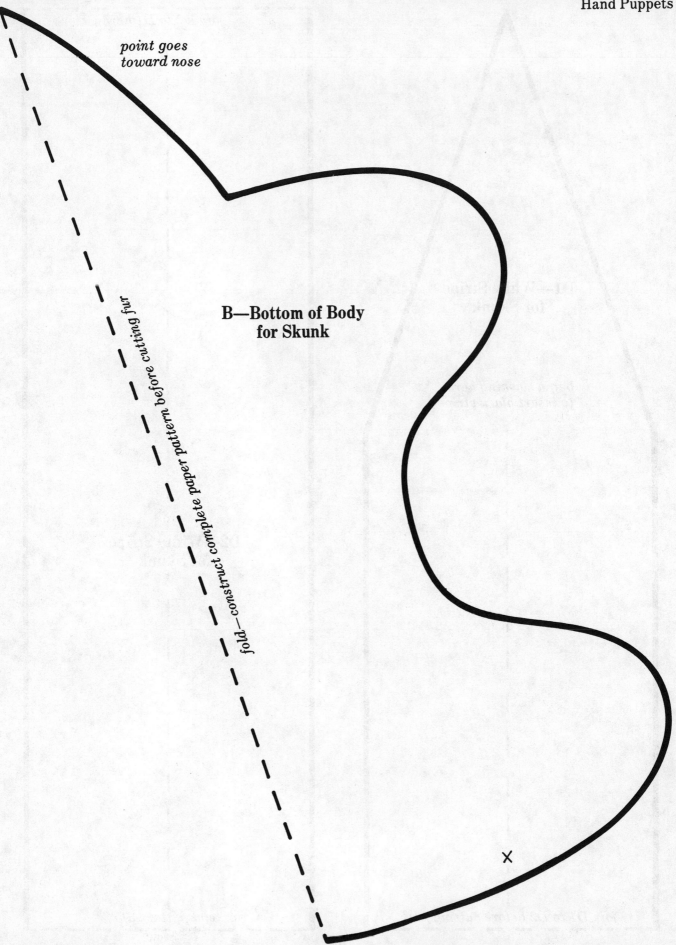

*point goes
toward nose*

B—Bottom of Body
for Skunk

fold—construct complete paper pattern before cutting fur

X

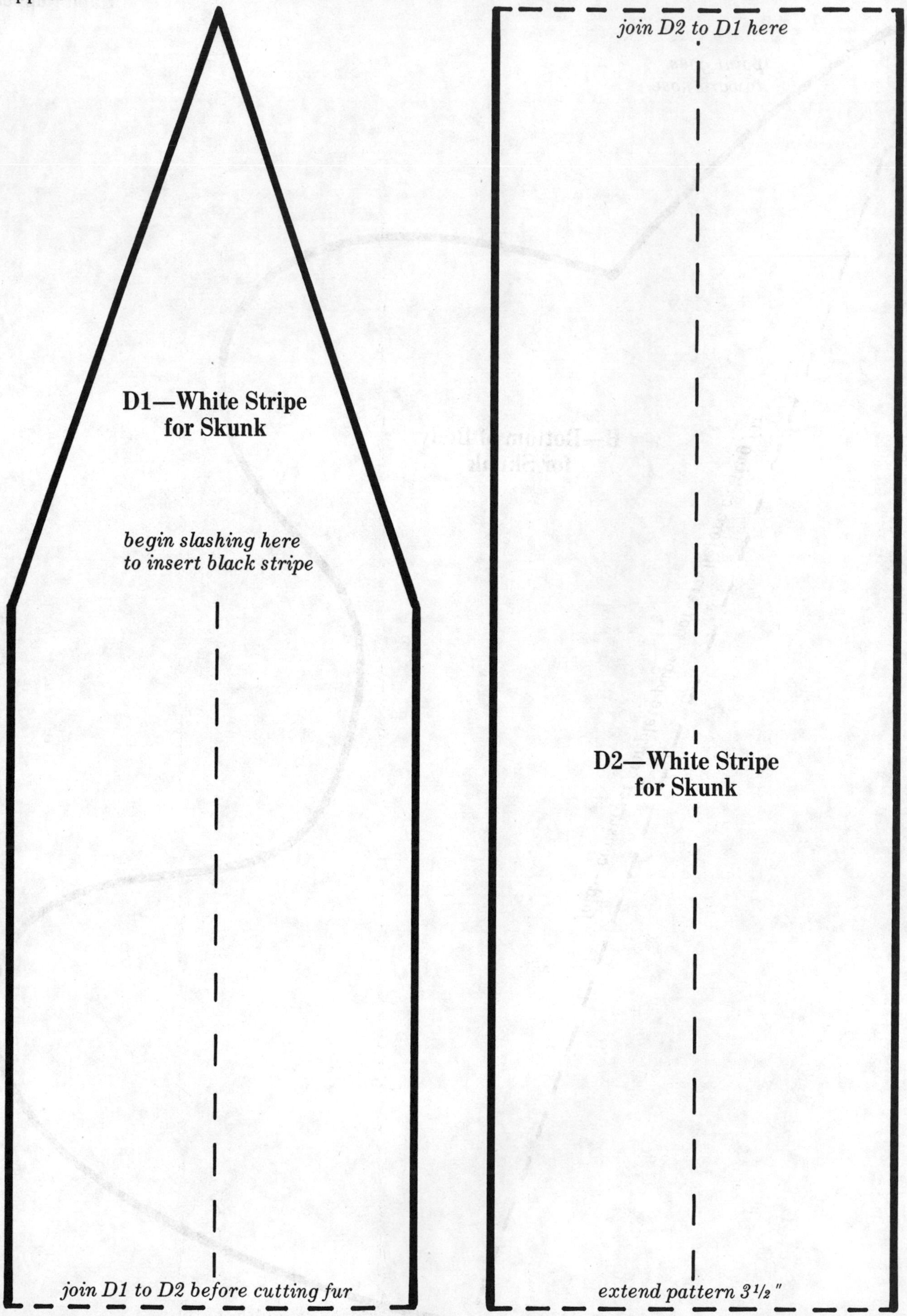

**D1—White Stripe
for Skunk**

*begin slashing here
to insert black stripe*

join D2 to D1 here

**D2—White Stripe
for Skunk**

join D1 to D2 before cutting fur

extend pattern 3½"

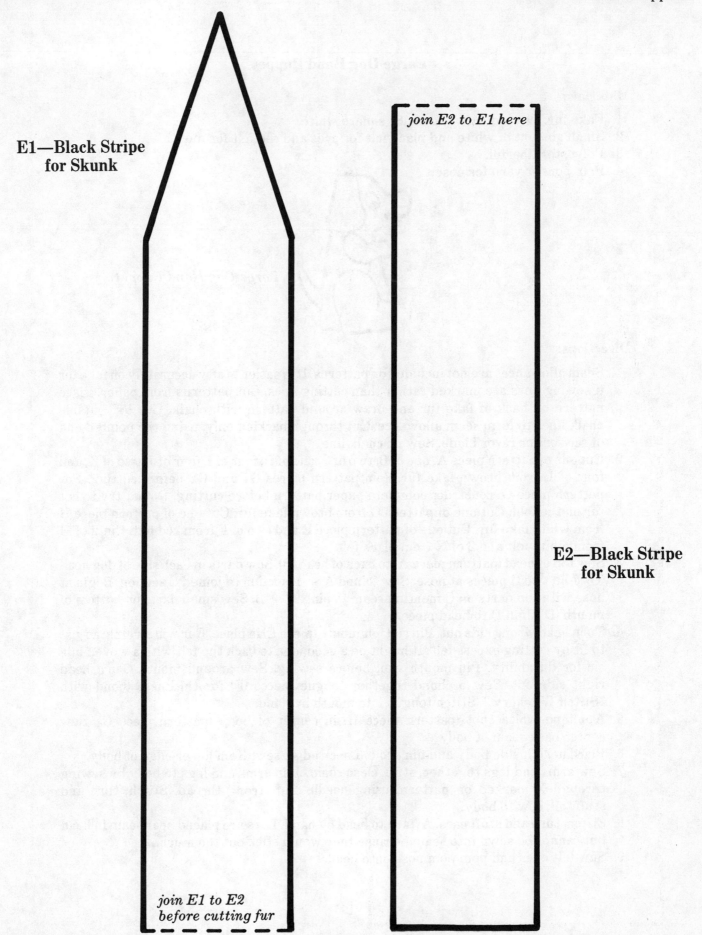

**E1—Black Stripe
for Skunk**

join E2 to E1 here

**E2—Black Stripe
for Skunk**

*join E1 to E2
before cutting fur*

195

Large Dog Hand Puppet

Materials:

1. Fake fur: ½ yard dark brown; 8″ square white.
2. Small amount of white and black felt for eyes and red felt for mouth.
3. Polyester fiberfill.
4. Pom pom or yarn for nose.

Large Dog Hand Puppet

Directions:

1. Seam allowances are not included on patterns. It is easier to sew accurately on fake fur if sewing lines are marked rather than cutting lines. Cut patterns from paper. Place pattern on back of fake fur and draw around pattern with chalk. Cut ½″ outside chalk lines to form seam allowance. Cut through backing only, using the pointed end of scissors or razor blade. Sew on chalk line.
2. Cut one of pattern piece A, one of B, two of C, one of D, four of I, four of J, two of K, and four of L from brown fake fur. Join pattern pieces G1 and G2 before cutting. For pattern piece G, construct complete paper pattern before cutting. Do not try to cut fur on the fold. Cut one of pattern G from brown fake fur. Cut one of pattern piece H from white fake fur. Cut one of pattern piece E and two of F from red felt. Cut 2 of M from white felt and 2 of N from black felt.
3. Sew top of head (pattern piece A) to back of head (B). Sew darts in each side of dog head (C). Join two C pieces at nose. Sew joined A + B section to joined C section. Begin at nose with top darts on C meeting seam joining A + B. Sew small darts on bottom of mouth (D). Join D to head piece.
4. Turn head wrong side out. Pin red felt mouth (piece E) in place. Fur will stretch; adjust to fit by cutting excess felt. It might be a good idea to back the felt with a woven fabric for durability. Pin mouth well before sewing. Sew around mouth. Turn head right side out. Sew or bond together tongue pieces (F) for thickness (bond with "Stitch Witchery"). Stitch tongue into mouth by hand.
5. Applique white spot (pattern piece H) in center of body (pattern piece G). Sew center back seam of body.
6. Place head inside body and pin around neck edge, sew. Hem lower edge of body.
7. Sew arms and legs together, stuff, close seam. Join arms and legs to body by sewing through X marked on pattern, using needle and strong thread. Stitch, turn and stuff tail; sew to body.
8. Stitch, turn and stuff ears. Attach to head by hand. Ears are placed near seam in head but cannot be sewn into seam because they would stick out too much.
9. Sew felt eyes and pom pom nose onto head.

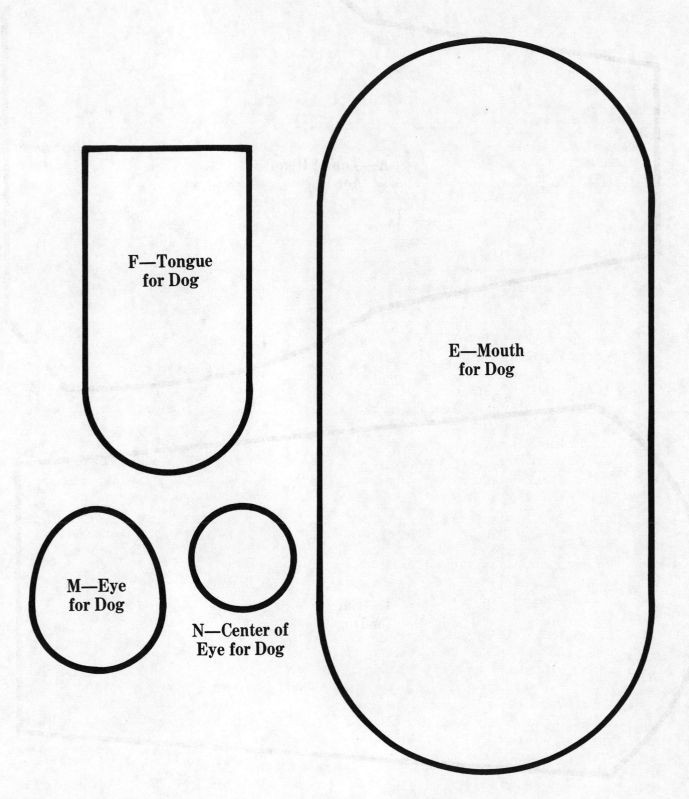

F—Tongue
for Dog

E—Mouth
for Dog

M—Eye
for Dog

N—Center of
Eye for Dog

197

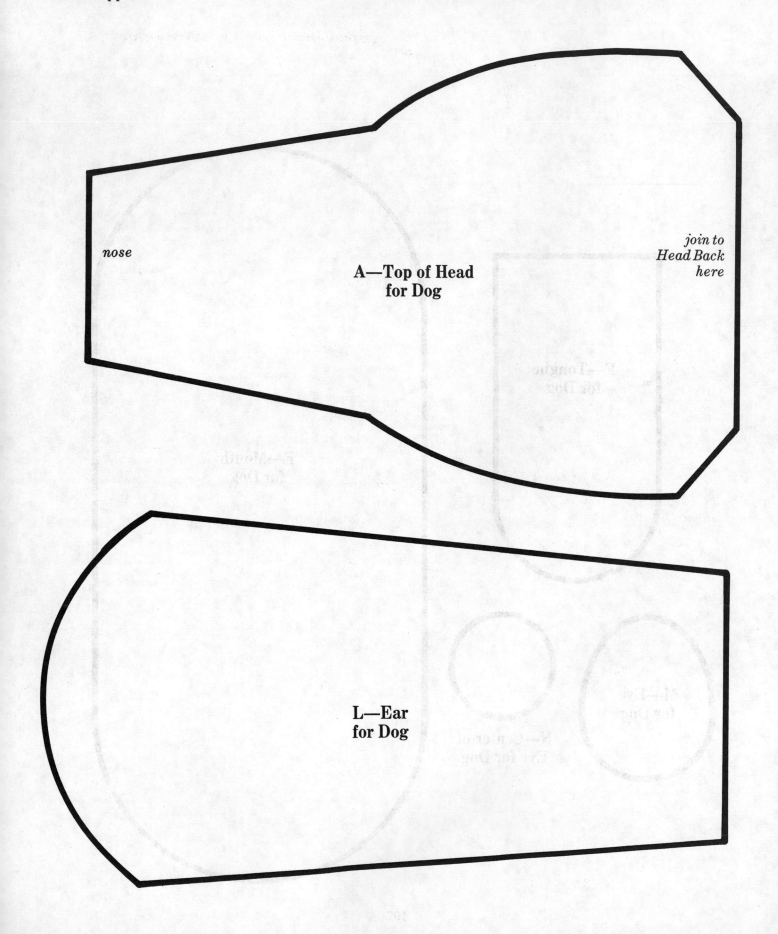

nose

**A—Top of Head
for Dog**

*join to
Head Back
here*

**L—Ear
for Dog**

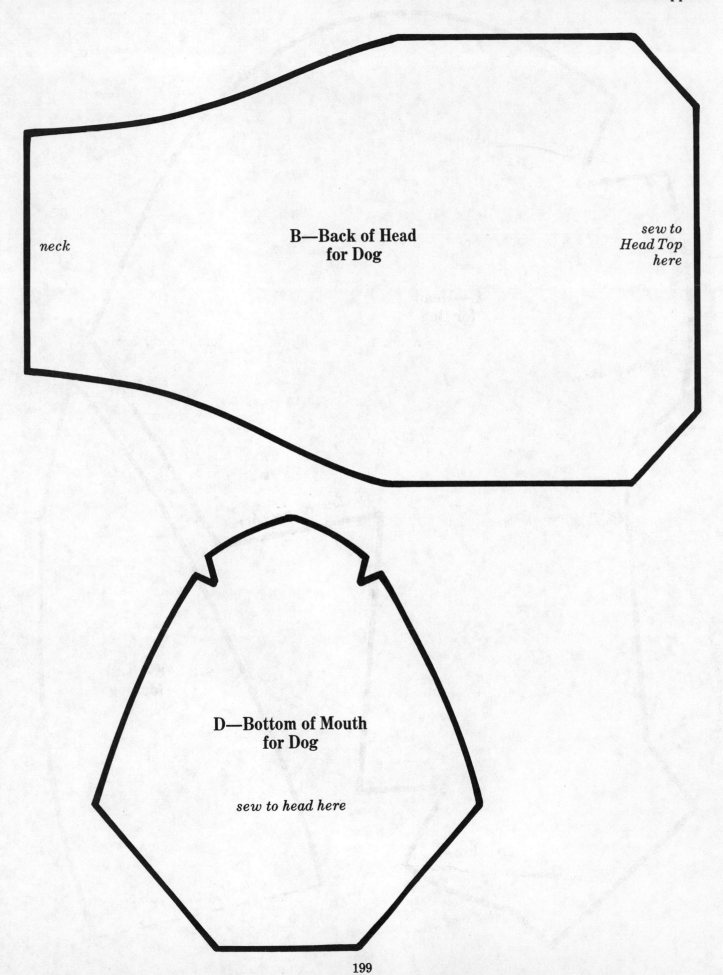

neck

B—Back of Head for Dog

sew to Head Top here

D—Bottom of Mouth for Dog

sew to head here

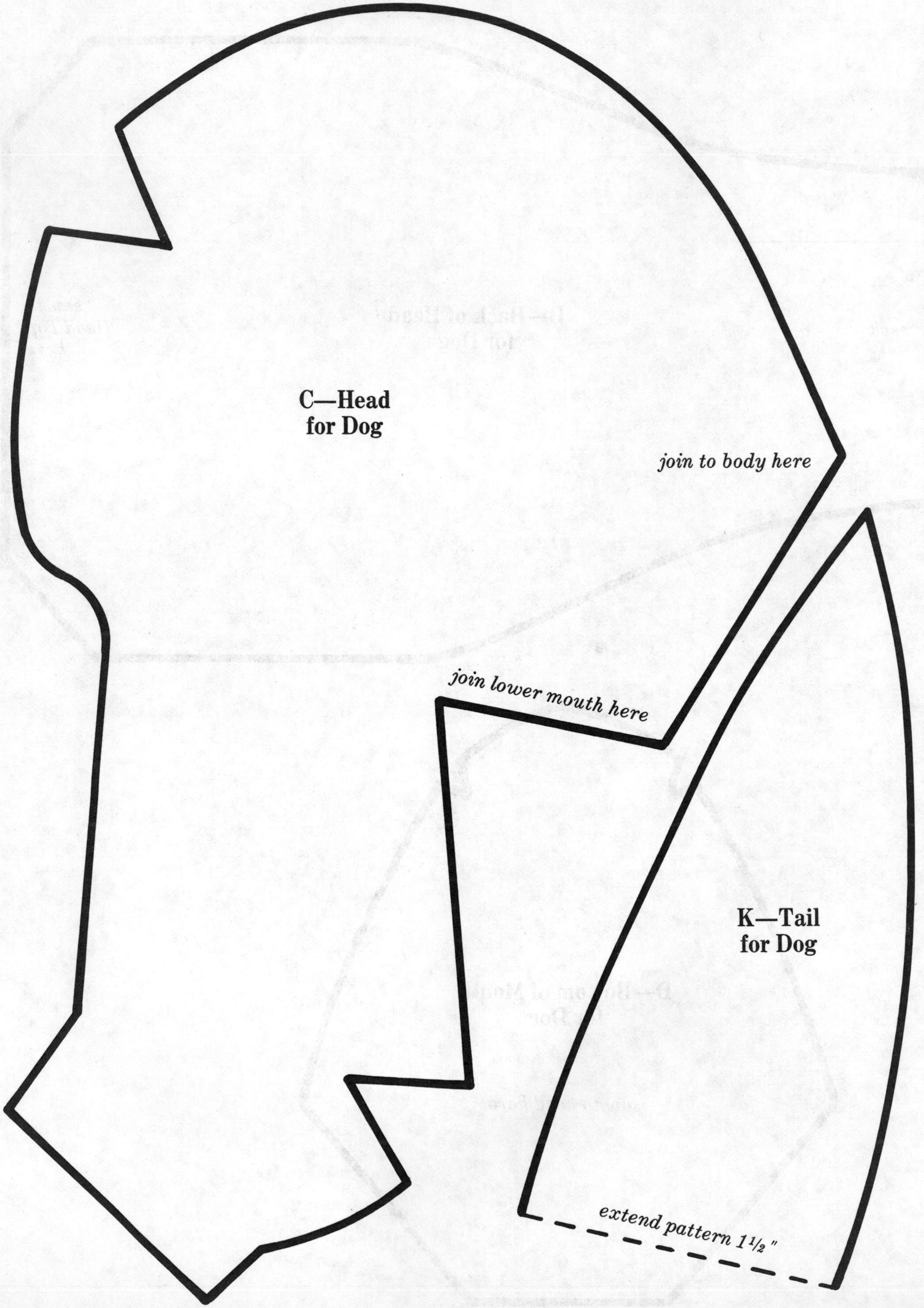

**C—Head
for Dog**

join to body here

join lower mouth here

**K—Tail
for Dog**

extend pattern 1½ "

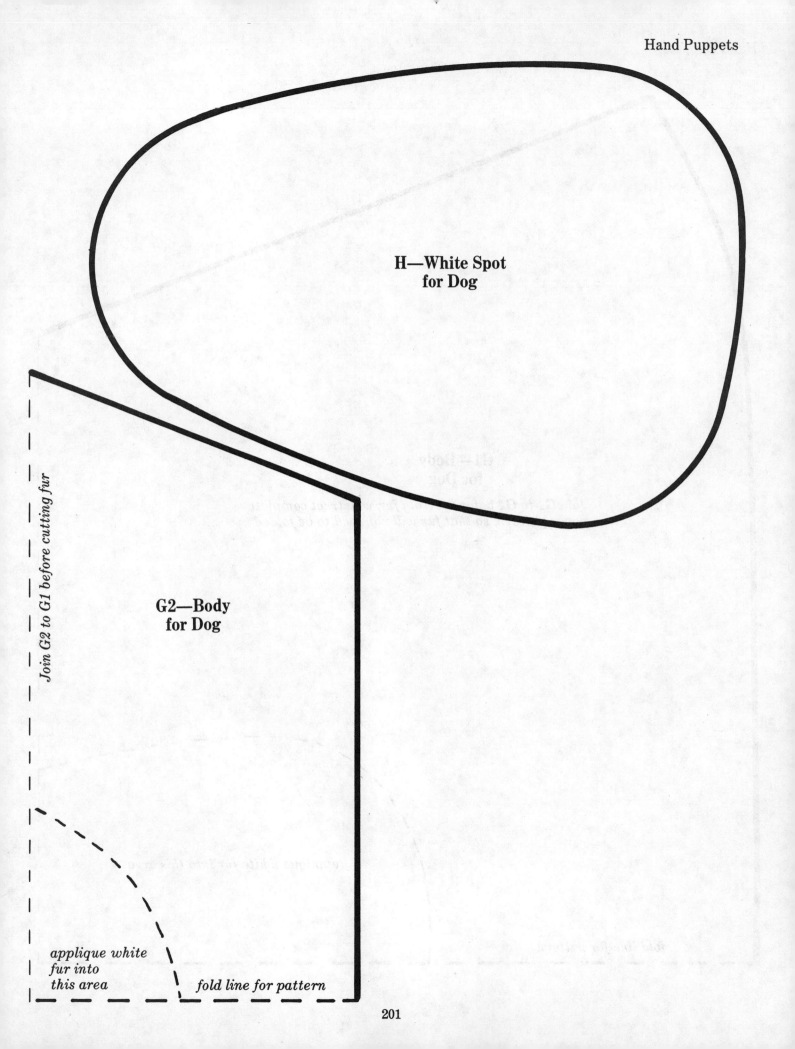

**H—White Spot
for Dog**

Join G2 to G1 before cutting fur

**G2—Body
for Dog**

*applique white
fur into
this area*

fold line for pattern

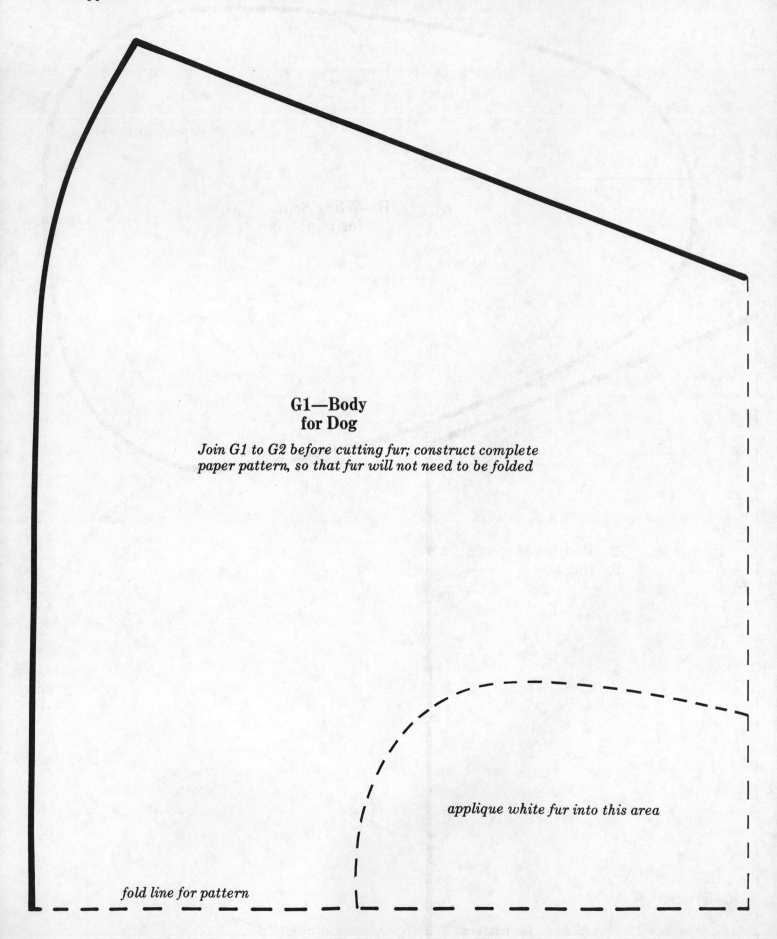

**G1—Body
for Dog**

*Join G1 to G2 before cutting fur; construct complete
paper pattern, so that fur will not need to be folded*

applique white fur into this area

fold line for pattern

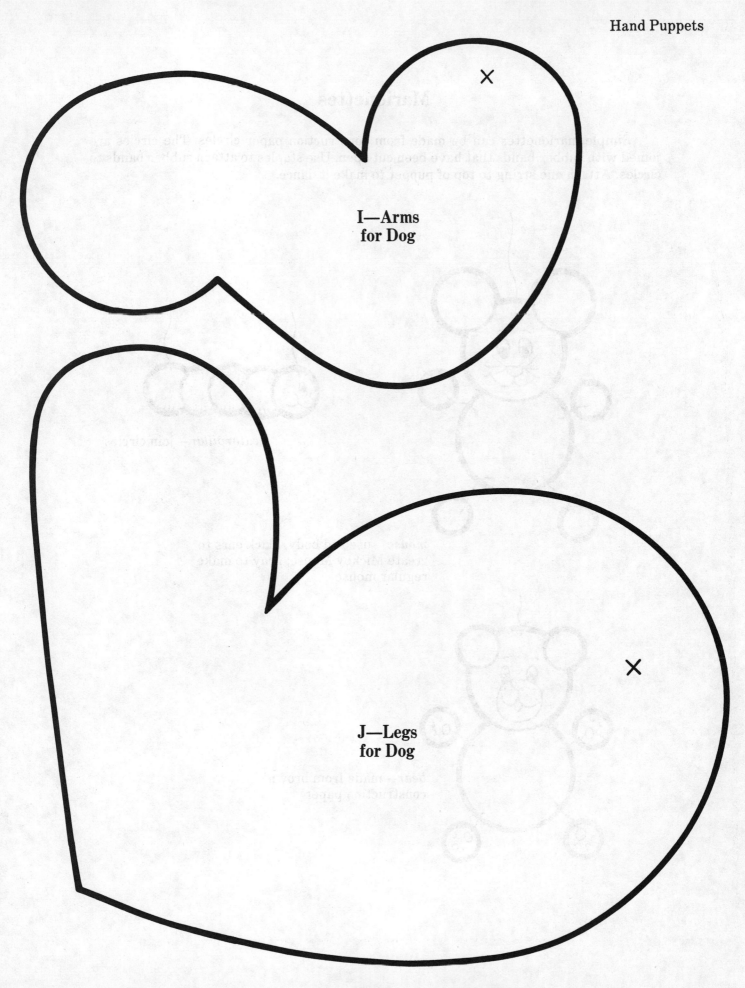

**I—Arms
for Dog**

**J—Legs
for Dog**

Marionettes

Simple marionettes can be made from construction paper circles. The circles are joined with rubber bands that have been cut open. Use staples to attach rubber bands to circles. Attach one string to top of puppet to make it dance.

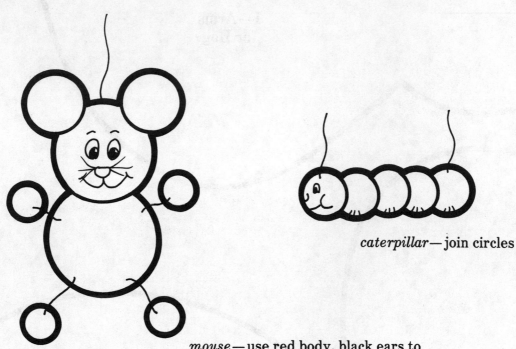

caterpillar—join circles

mouse—use red body, black ears to create Mickey Mouse; gray to make regular mouse

bear—made from brown construction paper

Poster Board Marionette

Materials:

1. Poster board for body, arms, and legs.
2. Yarn for hair.
3. Paper fasteners.
4. Pom poms for buttons.
5. String.

Directions:

1. Cut out one body, two arms, and two legs.
2. Decorate with colored markers, add yarn hair.
3. Glue on pom poms for buttons.
4. Punch hole for string through top of head, holes in body for arms and legs, and at top of arms and legs.
5. Join body to arms and legs with paper fasteners.
6. Run string through hole at top of head.

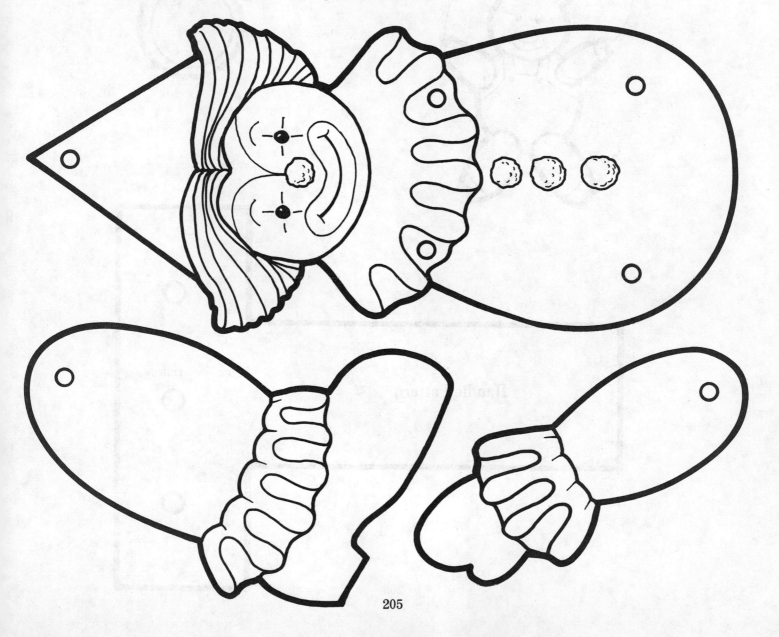

Three-String Puppets (pig, wolf, dog)

General Directions:

1. Cut bodies, arms, legs, and handles from ¼″ wood.
2. Drill holes in bodies, arms, legs and handles where needed for rivets and strings.
3. Sand and paint bodies, arms, and legs with acrylic paints.
4. Rivet arms and legs to body.
5. Attach strings to puppet and to cafe curtain rings of handle.

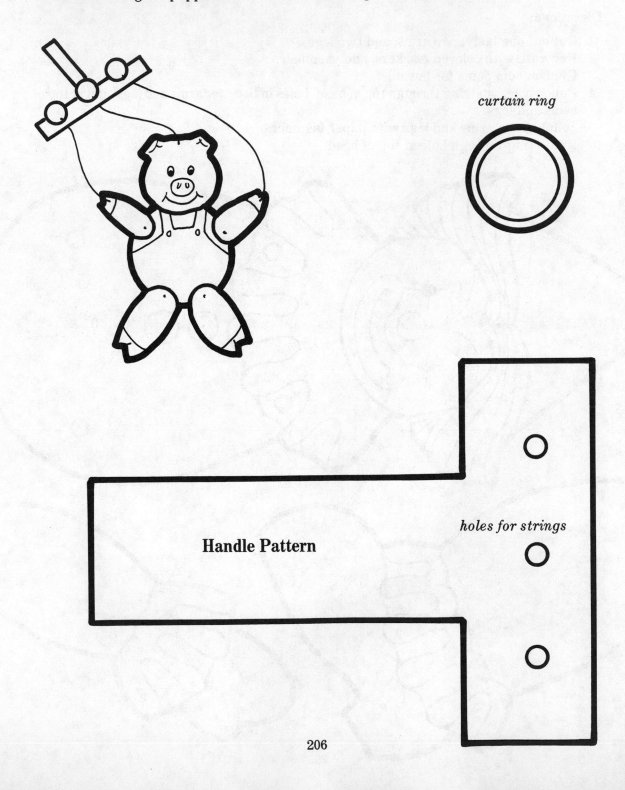

curtain ring

holes for strings

Handle Pattern

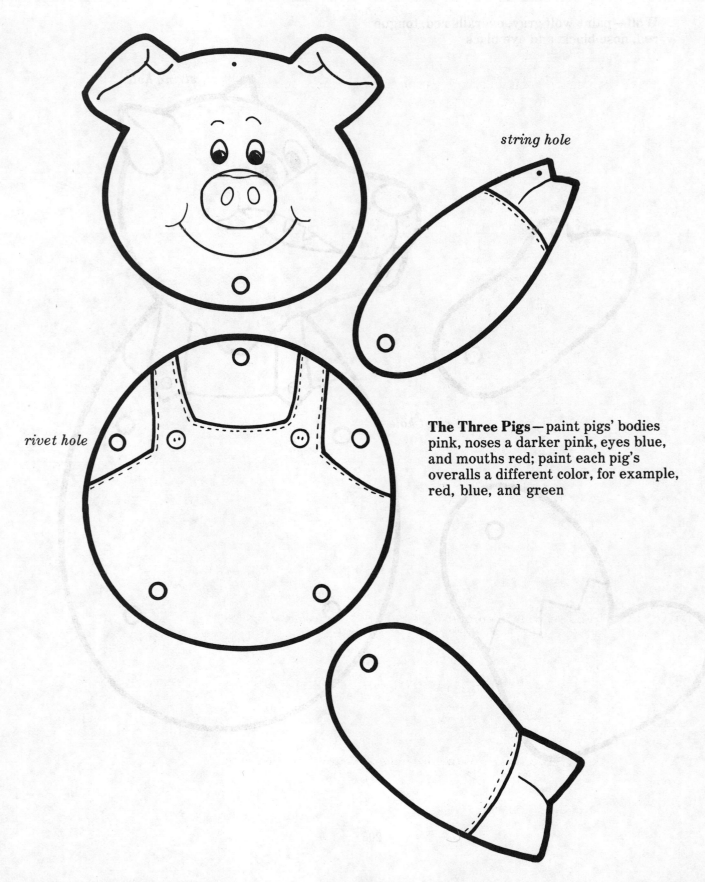

string hole

rivet hole

The Three Pigs—paint pigs' bodies pink, noses a darker pink, eyes blue, and mouths red; paint each pig's overalls a different color, for example, red, blue, and green

Wolf — paint wolf gray, overalls red, tongue red, nose black, and eye black

string hole

rivet hole

Dog

string hole

rivet hole

Large Marionette

Materials:

- *Marionette Body*
  1. ¾ ″ wood for body and handle.
  2. ¼ ″ dowel rods to join pieces of body.
  3. Small eyelets, rubber plumbing washers.
- *Marionette Head*
  1. 5″ styrofoam ball for head.
  2. 1″ styrofoam ball for nose and ears
     (½ ball forms nose; ¼ forms ear).
  3. ½ ″ dowel rod, 5½ ″ long.
  4. 2 small screw eyes.
  5. Pariscraft or papier-mache.
  6. Acrylic paints; modeling paste (optional).
  7. Fake fur for hair.
  8. Glue, straight pins.
- *Marionette Clothing*
  1. Fabric.
  2. Narrow elastic.
  3. Rick rack.
  4. Pre-gathered ruffled trim (you could also
     make a ruffle by gathering a 12″ x 2″
     strip of fabric).
  5. Trims to decorate clothing—pom poms for
     clown, patches for hobo, etc.

Large Marionette

Directions:

- *Marionette Body*
  1. *Note:* A jig saw or band saw is required to construct the large marionette.
  2. Draw pattern pieces (see pages 214 and 215) on ¾ ″ wood and cut with a power saw. Cut one of body; two each of top leg, bottom leg, top arm, bottom arm, hands and feet. Extend pattern for handle as noted on pattern; cut one. Sand pieces after cutting.
  3. Use small wooden dowel rods to join legs, arms, and hands (wooden Q-tip sticks may also be used).
  4. Drill holes through each of the sections of the body, legs, and arms that have U-shaped endings. These holes should be the same size as the small dowel rods.
  5. Drill a slightly larger hole through all pieces that fit into the U-shaped ending. Insert and glue dowels at each side of the U-shaped piece. *Note:* It is easier to attach hands after dressing marionette.
  6. Attach arms to body with nails (nail must not be long enough to enter neck area). To do this, drill a hole in top of each arm slightly larger than nail. Drill a larger hole on top of that hole from the outside of the arm about ¼ ″ into the arm (countersink). The larger hole will conceal the head of the nail and prevent the nail from catching on puppet clothing.

7. Place a rubber plumbing washer between arm and body to maintain space for clothing.

8. Use two ¼" dowel rods approximately 1½" long to attach feet to body. Drill a hole through feet and bottom of legs the size of dowel rod. Put glue in holes and bottom of leg section. Clamp together until dry. (Excess dowel may be cut off after glue is dry.)

- *Marionette Head* (see illustrations on page 212)

1. To form crease for cheeks and nose, hold styrofoam ball on edge of table and press firmly. Rotate ball until crease extends a little less than half way around head. Smooth forehead by gently rolling ball on table.

2. Attach ¼ of a 1" styrofoam ball to side of head for ears. Use straight pins and glue to hold ears in place. Ears may be shaped slightly with fingers.

3. Attach ½ of 1" styrofoam ball for nose. Crush slightly if desired.

4. To attach neck to head, insert the 5½" piece of dowel rod through the middle of the shaped head. The puppet will have more personality if the dowel is slightly off center, so do not attempt to be too exact. Insert the dowel slowly. Remove it occasionally if styrofoam begins to crumble and remove chips of styrofoam; insert dowel again and continue pressing until hole is formed from top to bottom of head.

5. Remove dowel; insert screw eye in each end of dowel; add glue to hole in ball; reinsert dowel. (Small eye at neck attaches head to body; eye at top of head attaches string from control handle.) Small chips of styrofoam missing from the center hole will not show after head is covered.

6. Use Pariscraft to cover head. Pariscraft is a fabric covered with plaster manufactured by the Johnson and Johnson Company. It is available at craft stores. Papier-mache may be used instead. Cut small pieces of Pariscraft, dip into water, and place on head. Cover head with at least two layers. Make the area that will be the face as smooth as possible. After covering head, allow to dry overnight. Rest head in a glass to dry, with rim of glass touching part that will be covered by hair.

7. Paint head with modeling paste for a smoother finish (this is optional). Then paint entire head and neck with acrylic paint. Paint features with acrylics (permanent markers could also be used for details).

8. Attach hair. To prevent a raw edge of fur showing around puppet's face, turn under fake fur around face. Hold face on lap; place edge of fur on hair line with right side down against head. The right side of the hair will be over the face. Pin straight pins about 2" apart across hair line. A hammer may be needed to insert pins. Place glue on head; turn hair from face onto head. It is helpful to place a safety pin through hair into eyelet at the top of dowel rod so eyelet will be easy to find when stringing puppet to controls.

9. Join head to body after head is completed. Screw small eyelets into body and dowel that goes into head.

Marionette Head

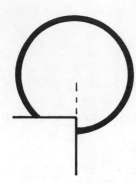  

*shape styrofoam
ball by pressing
over table edge*

*place eyes
in dowel rod*

*insert and glue dowel
into shaped ball*

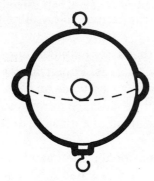  

*pin and glue ears
and nose to ball*

*cover ball with
Pariscraft or papier-mache*

*paint head with acrylic
paints; use permanent
markers for details—
red mouth, blue eyes,
pink circles on cheeks,
outline with black marker*

*pin fake fur with
right side down to
head; turn hair over
back of head and glue*

completed head

- *Marionette Clothing*

1. Cut 4 of pattern piece from fabric.
2. Stitch center front beginning at neck and ending 7″ from bottom (points A to B).
3. Stitch center back beginning 5″ below neck and ending 7″ from bottom (from below point A to B; leave 5″ open for dressing puppet).
4. Stitch side seams from beneath arm to bottom of leg (points C to D).
5. Stitch shoulder seams to within 1″ of neck (points E to F).
6. Stitch inside leg seam (points G to B).
7. Stitch elastic around ends of arms and legs (1½″ from edges). Elastic may be stitched directly to fabric by stretching while sewing, or may be inserted through a casing made of bias tape.
8. Narrow-hem edges of legs and arms. Trim with rick rack.
9. Sew ruffle around neck.
10. Decorate clothing as desired.

- *Finishing Marionette*

1. Drill small holes into puppet to hold clear fishing line — a hole at each shoulder, a hole in each thumb, a hole in each knee (**not foot**), and a hole in the bottom of the body (seat).
2. Insert clear fishing line into each hole. Tie about five knots on top of each other at each end of the fishing line. (Fishing line is slippery, so knots work out if they are not tied several times. Fishing line is almost invisible, so it is used rather than thread.)
3. Dress puppet, then use a large-eyed needle to thread fishing line through clothing into puppet handle. Use round cafe curtain rings in the puppet handle. Tie line securely again.

Pattern for Marionette Clothing

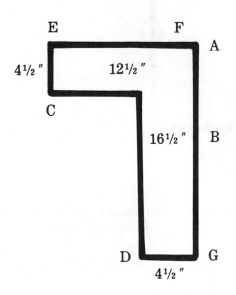

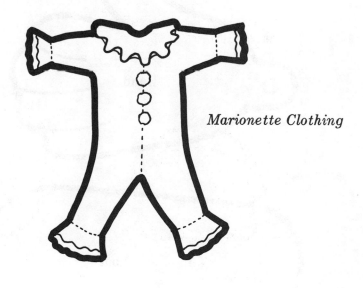

Marionette Clothing

Patterns for Body of Large Marionette

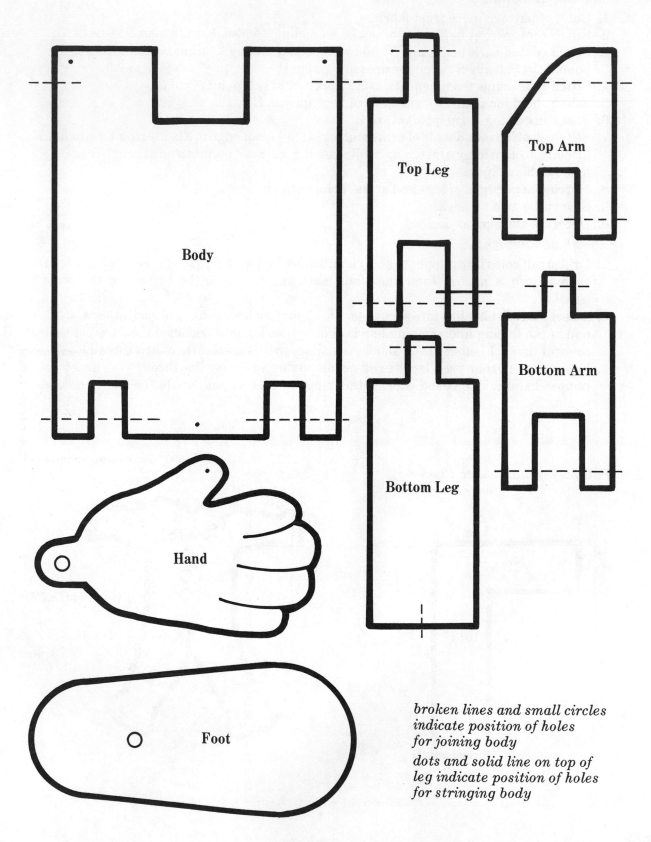

Body

Top Leg

Top Arm

Bottom Arm

Bottom Leg

Hand

Foot

*broken lines and small circles
indicate position of holes
for joining body*

*dots and solid line on top of
leg indicate position of holes
for stringing body*

Control Handle for Large Marionette

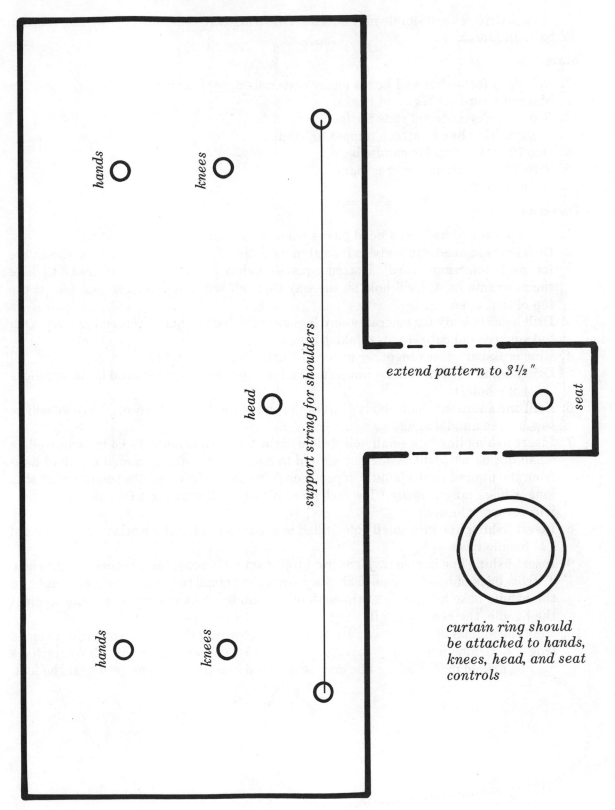

hands

knees

head

support string for shoulders

extend pattern to 3½"

seat

curtain ring should
be attached to hands,
knees, head, and seat
controls

hands

knees

"Crazy Critters"

Crazy Critters are simple marionettes. All strings are controlled by rocking the handle back and forth.

Materials:

1. ¾" wood for bodies and heads (other materials may be substituted for the wood).
2. Macrame cord for legs and necks.
3. Broomsticks or dowel rods for feet.
4. Clear fishing line to attach puppet to handle.
5. One 12" x 1" strip for handle base.
6. Two 10" x 1" strips for crossbars.
7. Acrylic paint.

Directions:

1. Cut one each of body and head pieces from ¾" wood. Cut four feet. Sand.
2. Drill holes in head and body as indicated by dotted lines on patterns. These holes are for neck (macrame cord). Dotted squares indicate countersinking areas to hide the macrame knot. Drill hole all the way through head, then drill larger hole at the top of that opening.
3. Drill holes in body for macrame cord legs as indicated by small circles on pattern. Dotted squares indicate countersinking areas.
4. Glue crossbar pieces together (refer to illustration on page 217).
5. Drill a small hole for fishing line at the end of each piece of wood used in the handle (a total of 6 holes).
6. Drill one additional hole about 4" from the end of the 12" base piece. (This hole will be toward the animal's tail.)
7. Insert fishing line into small hole drilled in the top back of animal's body (indicated by small dot on pattern). Attach other end to back of 12" handle base. (Length of lines from the puppet to the handle depends on personal preference, but keep in mind that longer lines tangle easily.) Tie each piece of fishing line at least four times so knots will not work loose.
8. Insert fishing line into small hole drilled in animal's head. Attach other end to front of 12" handle base.
9. Insert fishing line in hole towards front top of animal's body. Insert other end into hole 4" from back of handle base. (This line allows the animal to "eat.") Run your finger up the handle base beginning at the back of the handle. As you move the string against the handle, the head will fall.
10. Hold the animal up and make sure you have each string the length you need. Insert a length of fishing line in each foot and attach it to the crossbar directly above it. Holes may be drilled in feet or the line may be inserted into the macrame cord near the foot.

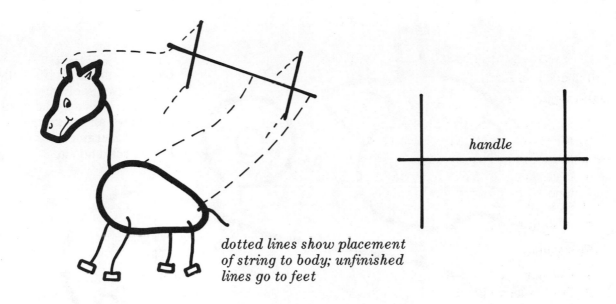

dotted lines show placement of string to body; unfinished lines go to feet

handle

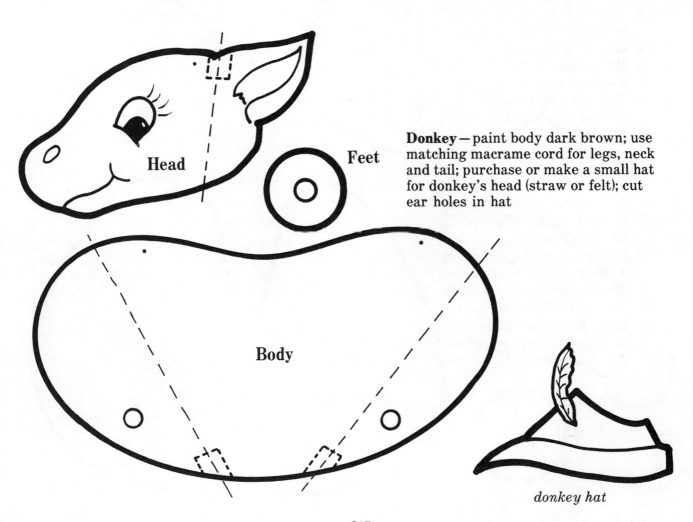

Head

Feet

Donkey—paint body dark brown; use matching macrame cord for legs, neck and tail; purchase or make a small hat for donkey's head (straw or felt); cut ear holes in hat

Body

donkey hat

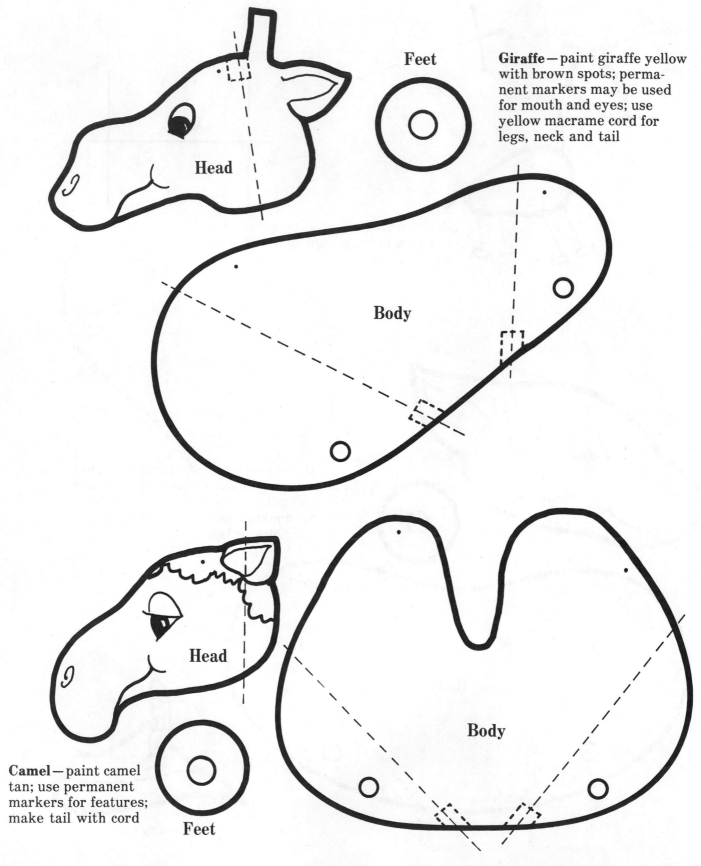

Feet

Head

Giraffe—paint giraffe yellow with brown spots; permanent markers may be used for mouth and eyes; use yellow macrame cord for legs, neck and tail

Body

Head

Body

Camel—paint camel tan; use permanent markers for features; make tail with cord

Feet

218

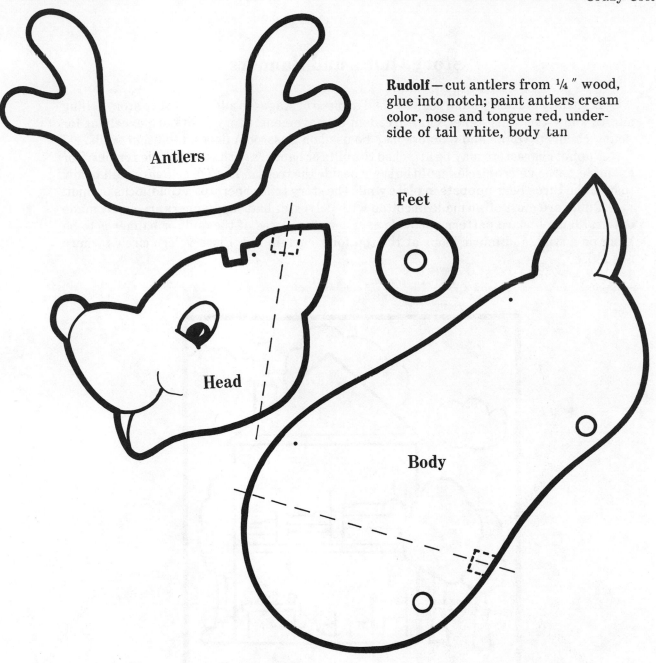

Rudolf—cut antlers from ¼″ wood, glue into notch; paint antlers cream color, nose and tongue red, underside of tail white, body tan

Antlers

Feet

Head

Body

Simplified Crazy Critter (construction paper lion)

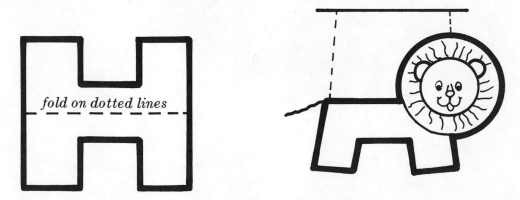

fold on dotted lines

219

Story Quilts and Banners

A variety of backgrounds can be used in place of stages to add interest to story telling and to allow the story teller more freedom of movement. Story quilts are excellent for young children. Quilts and banners may be used on classroom floors, tables, or walls.

Puppet characters may be attached to quilts or banners with velcro circles or ties. For example, three velcro circles could be sewn beside the trees in *The Three Bears* quilt below to hold the three bear puppets in place while the story teller operates a Goldilocks puppet.

Quilts are most often made of cotton with polyester batting. Banners are easily made of felt. Flannel board patterns provide excellent resources. If the quilt or banner is to be hung on a wall, add fabric loops at the top for a curtain rod. Place velcro circles where needed.

Story Telling Quilt

Story Telling Aprons

Story telling aprons are especially convenient for story tellers who move from classroom to classroom or from group to group within a classroom. The story teller who likes to gather listeners outdoors under a tree might find the apron very useful. The apron serves as the background for the story in the same way a flannel board or puppet stage might be used. The lower pocket of the apron serves to hold the characters or props for the story.

"The Mitten" — Apron and Finger Puppets

Materials for Apron:

1. Light blue washable fabric for apron.
2. Assorted cotton fabrics for appliqued decorations: yellow for sun, green for tree tops, brown for tree trunks, white for snow mountain and for pocket. (If the apron will not be washed, felt may be used.)
3. Embroidery floss for details.

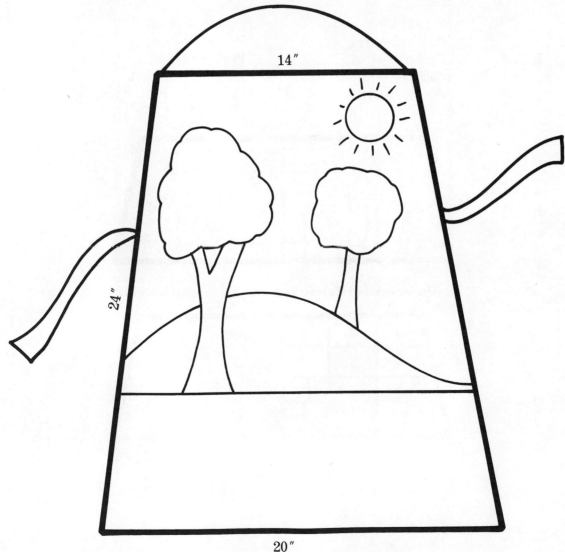

Directions for Apron:

1. Cut apron to dimensions shown in illustration on page 221. These dimensions include ½ʺ seam allowances.
2. Narrow-hem edges of apron.
3. Cut piece for neck strap. Fold in raw edges lengthwise; stitch. Stitch to apron.
4. Applique scene on apron. Lines shown on patterns are cutting lines. If using cotton, turn under raw edges when appliqueing. If using felt, edge will not need to be turned under. Use embroidery thread to create rays of sun.
5. Cut out pocket for apron. Apron pocket may be made from one piece of fabric sewn to the bottom and sides of the apron and stitched up the middle to prevent sagging. Props and characters could then be stored in both sides of the pocket.
6. Pocket may also be elaborately constructed to hold each character in its own place. This allows the story teller to reach into the pocket without interrupting the story to look for each character. A simple pocket may be used on placed on top of the elaborate pocket to conceal it, or to hold the script and additional props. The pocket shown below was constructed to accompany the Ukranian folktale, *The Mitten* (see page 232). The characters are placed in each pocket in the order that they appear in the story:

Pocket 1 — mouse	Pocket 6 — wolf
Pocket 2 — frog	Pocket 7 — boar
Pocket 3 — owl	Pocket 8 — bear
Pocket 4 — rabbit	Pocket 9 — cricket
Pocket 5 — fox	Pocket 10 — mitten and script

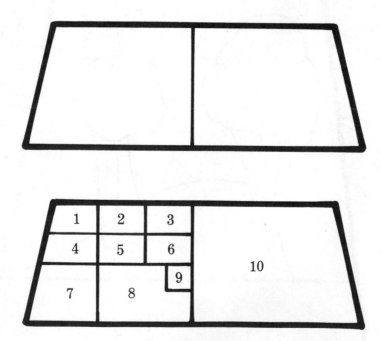

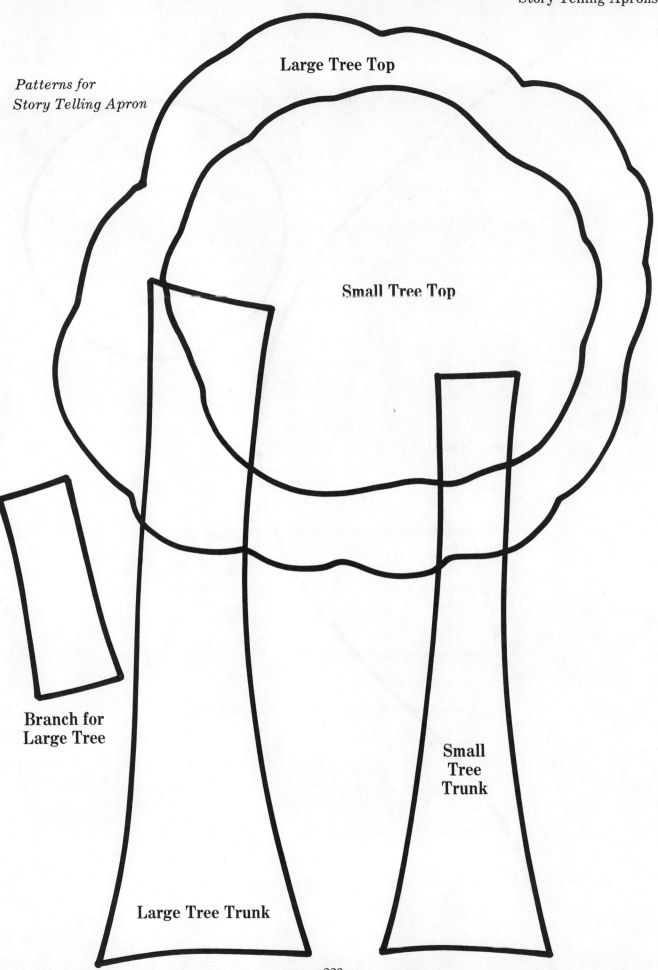

Large Tree Top

*Patterns for
Story Telling Apron*

Small Tree Top

Branch for
Large Tree

Small
Tree
Trunk

Large Tree Trunk

Story Telling Aprons

Patterns for Story Telling Apron

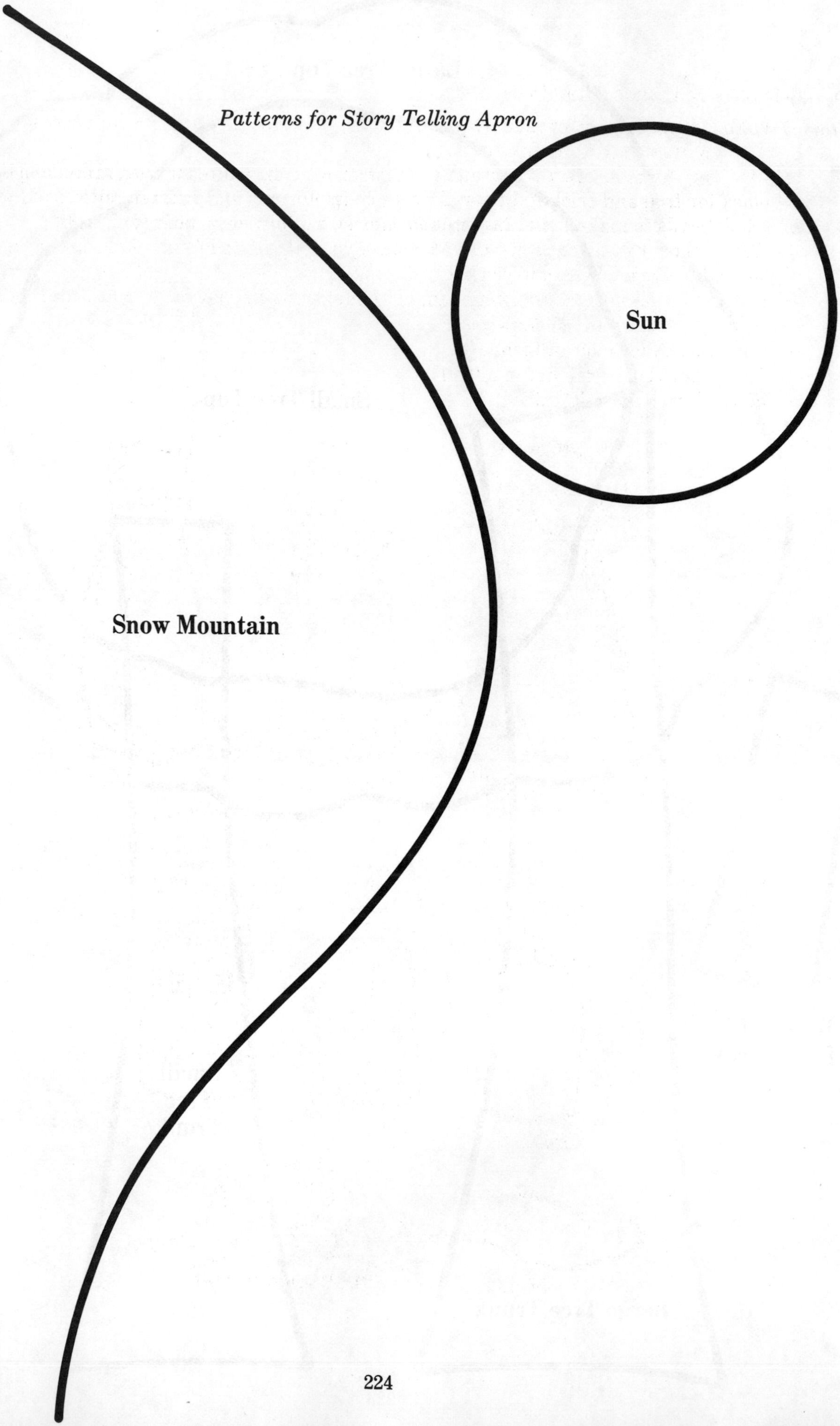

Sun

Snow Mountain

Materials for Finger Puppets:

1. Fake fur fabric: gray for mouse, boar and wolf; white for rabbit; beige for bear and fox, color as desired to trim mitten.
2. Felt: gray for mouse, owl, boar and wolf; green for frog; white for frog, rabbit and boar; black for frog and cricket; brown for owl; beige for owl and fox; red for fox and wolf.
3. Black beads to make facial features for mouse, rabbit, bear, boar, fox, wolf.
4. Heavy black thread for whiskers for mouse and rabbit, and for cricket's antennae.
5. Moveable eyes for owl and cricket.
6. Pom poms: ½ ″ white for rabbit's tail; ¼ ″ pink for rabbit's nose; ¼ ″ white for rabbit's cheeks; ¼ ″ brown for bear's nose.
7. Pre-quilted fabric for mitten.
8. Red cotton flannel for lining mitten.
9. Velcro circles for mitten.

Bear   *Wolf*   *Boar*

Cricket

Rabbit   *Fox*   *Owl*

Frog

Mouse

Directions for Finger Puppets:

Note: Lines shown on patterns are **cutting** lines unless other noted. Use small seam allowances.

- *Mouse*
  1. Cut two of mouse body from gray fur, two of ear and one of tail from gray felt.
  2. Stitch body pieces together, leaving open between X's. Turn.
  3. Fold mouse ear in middle, sew to body. Sew tail to body.
  4. Eyes and nose of mouse are small black beads; whiskers are black thread.

- *Cricket*
  1. Cut two of cricket body, two of wings, and two each of legs from black felt.
  2. Stitch together body pieces, leaving open between X's.
  3. Glue on wings, legs, and small moveable eyes; add thread for antennae.

- *Owl*
  1. Cut two of owl body from brown felt, one of owl's eyes and two of wings from beige felt, and one of nose from gray felt.
  2. Stitch body pieces together on right side (do not turn), leaving bottom open.
  3. Glue eyes, nose, wings to body; glue moveable eyes on top of beige felt.

- *Rabbit*
  1. Cut two of rabbit body from white fur, two of rabbit ears from white felt.
  2. Stitch and turn rabbit body pieces, leaving bottom open.
  3. Sew on felt ears.
  4. Sew on ½ " pom pom for tail; cluster one ¼ " pink pom pom for nose and two ¼ " white pom poms for cheeks.
  5. Add beads for eyes; use heavy black thread for whiskers.

- *Frog*
  1. Cut two of frog body, one of head and two arms from green felt. Cut two eyes from white and black felt.
  2. Stitch body pieces together on right side (do not turn felt), leaving bottom open for fingers.
  3. Glue eyes to head, then glue head to body.
  4. Glue arms on top of body.

- *Bear*
  1. Cut two of bear body and one of muzzle from beige fur.
  2. Stitch and turn body pieces, leaving bottom open.
  3. Lines shown for legs and ears are sewing lines, not cutting lines. Place pattern on wrong side of fur and draw around it with marker. Sew pieces before cutting. Then cut out and sew to body.
  4. Sew muzzle to bear face, turning under raw edges.
  5. Use beads for eyes, ¼ " pom pom for nose.

• *Boar*
1. Cut two of boar body and one of boar snout from gray fur, two ears and end of snout from gray felt, tusks from white felt.
2. Stitch and turn body pieces, leaving bottom open.
3. For snout, fold gray fur crosswise. Sew around sides and curved top, leaving flat side open. Turn; hand-stitch flat side to face.
4. Glue on end of snout and tusks; use beads for eyes.

• *Fox*
1. Cut two of fox body and one of fox tail from beige fur; one of nose, two arms, two legs, and two ears from matching felt.
2. Sew body pieces together, leaving bottom open. Turn.
3. Gather along dashed line (see pattern) to form neck.
4. Fold tail and stitch around curved edges. Turn, stitch to body.
5. Stitch side A of nose to side B; then stitch to fox face.
6. Add arms, legs, and ears; use beads for eyes.

• *Wolf*
1. Cut two of wolf body from gray fur; one of nose, two arms, two legs, two ears and one tail from gray felt, one tongue from red felt.
2. Construct as fox, steps #2, #3, and #5.
3. Add arms, legs, ears, tail and tongue; use beads for eyes.

• *Mitten*
1. Cut two of quilted fabric, two of red cotton flannel for lining, and fur trim for cuff area.
2. Sew pieces of quilted fabric together between X marks (across finger portion of mitten).
3. On the other side of the X marks, sew flannel to quilted fabric, forming lining. Leave an opening for turning, hand-stitch opening closed.
4. After sewing, mitten will be joined across finger area, but unattached around thumb and heel of hand. Sew velcro circles about 2″ apart in the unattached area. This allows the mitten to come apart at the end of the story.
5. The mitten is constructed partially attached like this because the thickness of the quilted fabric created a bulky, "come apart" appearance if two separate halves were used. If the mitten is made of thinner fabric, it may be possible to simply use velcro to hold the two halves of the mitten together.

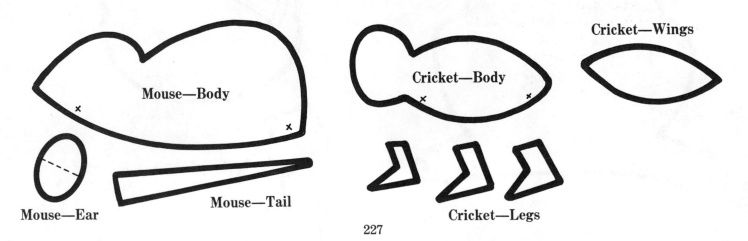

Mouse—Body

Cricket—Body

Cricket—Wings

Mouse—Ear

Mouse—Tail

Cricket—Legs

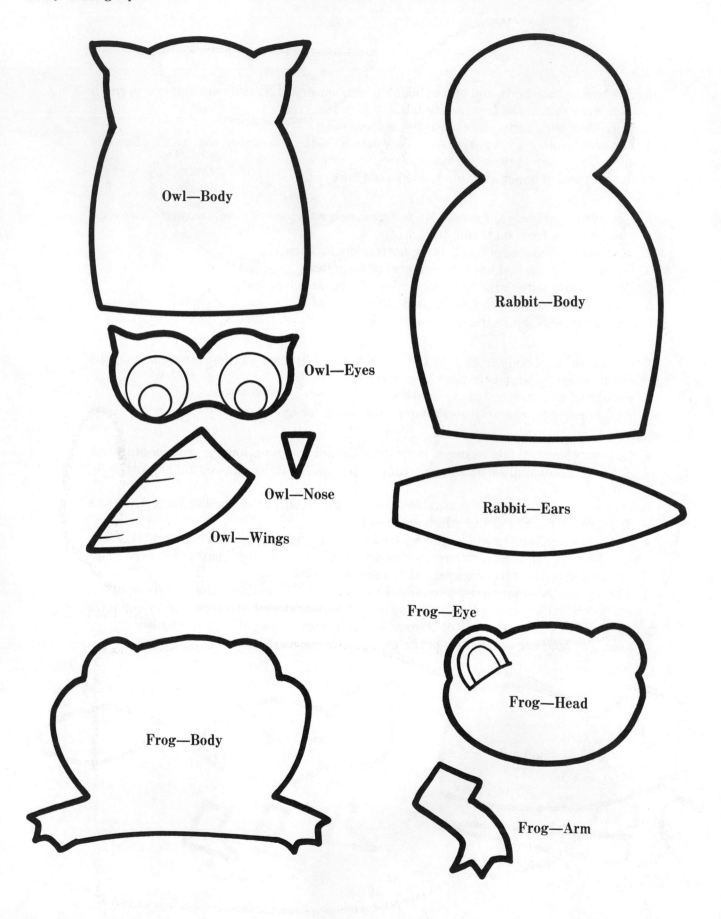

Owl—Body

Owl—Eyes

Owl—Nose

Owl—Wings

Rabbit—Body

Rabbit—Ears

Frog—Eye

Frog—Head

Frog—Body

Frog—Arm

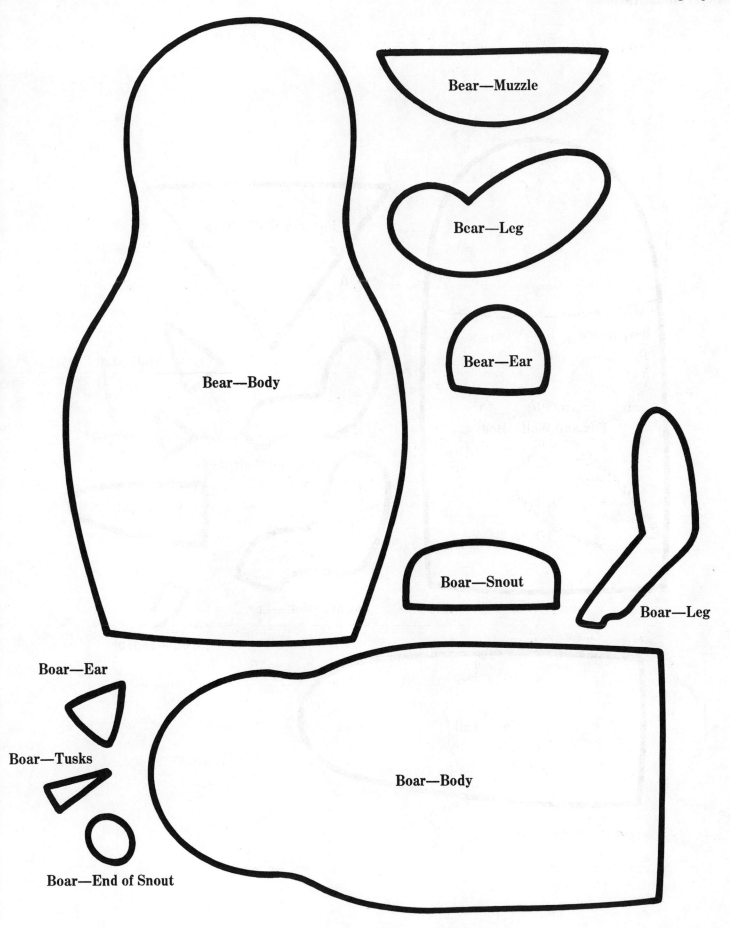

Bear—Muzzle

Bear—Leg

Bear—Ear

Bear—Body

Boar—Snout

Boar—Leg

Boar—Ear

Boar—Tusks

Boar—Body

Boar—End of Snout

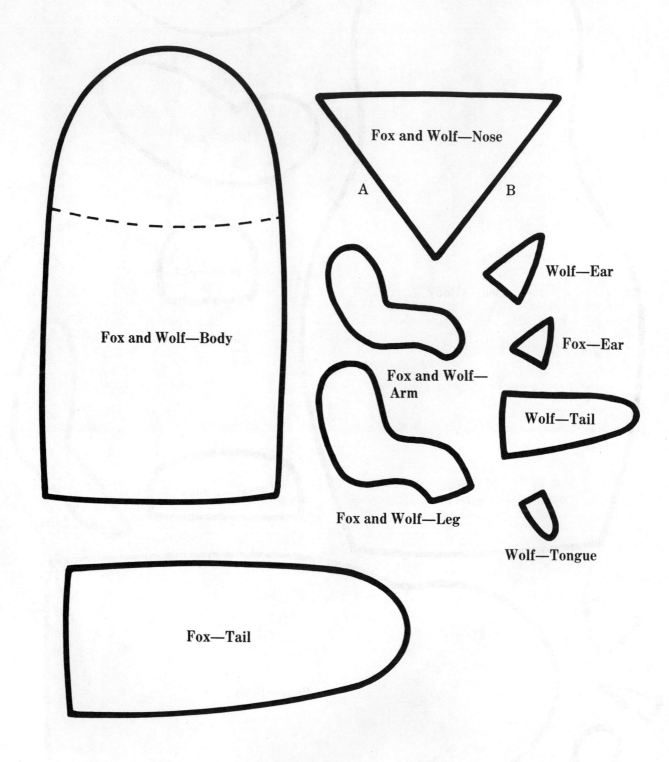

Fox and Wolf—Nose

A

B

Fox and Wolf—Body

Wolf—Ear

Fox—Ear

Fox and Wolf—Arm

Wolf—Tail

Fox and Wolf—Leg

Wolf—Tongue

Fox—Tail

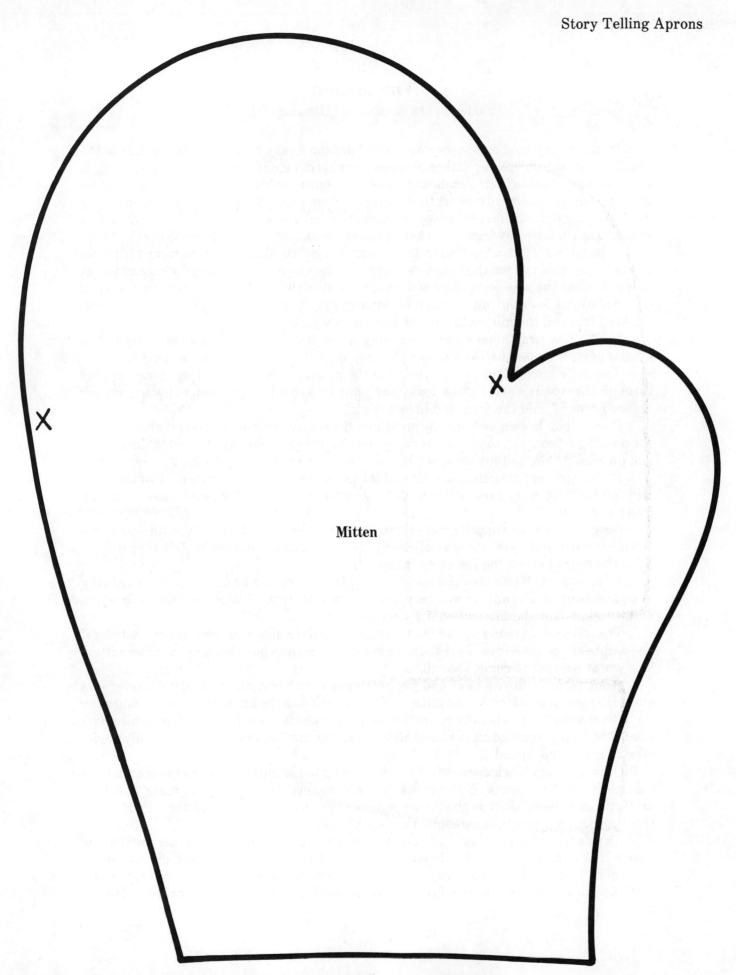

Mitten

The Mitten
A modern version of an old Ukranian folktale

It was a very cold and snowy day. The Simpson family had just used the last of the kindling for their fireplace. Father Simpson sent his daughter, Susy, to gather kindling in the wooded lot beside their farmhouse. Susy was a hard-working daughter, but she had one little problem—she really liked to daydream. Sometimes Susy got so involved in her daydreaming that she forget to pay attention to what she was supposed to be doing. She spent so much time daydreaming that her family nicknamed her "Spacey Susy."

"Spacey Susy" took her sled from the barn and pulled it behind her to carry the pieces of wood she gathered for the fireplace. Very soon, Susy was lost in a daydream and forget to watch what she was doing. One of her mittens fell off while she was arranging the wood on the sled and Susy did not even notice. Spacey Susy went on through the woods, gathering kindling, and the mitten lay on the cold, snowy ground.

Soon a tiny **gray mouse** came scurrying through the snow and saw the mitten. "Oh, what a perfect house that would make to keep me out of the cold," she squeaked.

The little mouse had just settled into the mitten when a **green frog** came hopping through the woods. "My, I think I will just jump into that little mitten and warm myself before I croak," said the frog, and in he hopped.

Presently a **brown owl** flew by and spied the mitten. "Whoo, whoo is there?" hooted the owl. "Can I come in, too?" Mouse really felt that three would be too many in the mitten, and owls made her awfully nervous, but she did want to share, so she let the owl enter.

It was not very long until a **white rabbit** came hopping by the mitten. "I will be very still and I will not make a sound if you will let me enter," whispered the rabbit as she hopped into the mitten.

Soon a **brown fox** came by and said to himself, "I am very sly. I bet I could sneak into the mitten without anyone even noticing." The other animals did notice, but they did not have the heart to turn the fox away in the cold.

A big **gray wolf** had seen the fox disappear into the mitten and decided she would try to squeeze in, too. The mitten was very full by then, and the wolf did a great deal of howling and wiggling, but she finally found a place in the mitten.

The mitten was really beginning to stretch, and the mouse was beginning to wonder if she had been too generous. Just then, a **gray boar** began to bore his way into the mitten. The worst was yet to come, though.

A big friendly **brown bear** had just wakened from hibernation, thinking winter was over. He came lumbering by the mitten. "Oh, no," cried all the animals. "You are much too big." "Nonsense," growled the bear. "I have been hibernating all winter. I am a nice trim size." The bear grumbled and twisted his way into the mitten. The mitten was really beginning to creak and squeak.

Outside a tiny **black cricket** had just limped up to the mitten. She was so old that the cold made her bones creak. With a creaky voice, she asked, "Please may I come in? I will not take up much room." Just as she began to put her skinny foot into the mitten, "POP" went the seams, and the mitten tore into a million pieces.

By this time, Spacey Susy had stopped daydreaming and noticed that her mitten was missing. On her way home she looked all around for the mitten, but she did not see it anywhere. She did see a funny gray mouse with a piece of red fabric on her head that looked just like the lining of the mitten. Spacey Susy never did really know what happened to her mitten.

Puppet Stages

cardboard boxes—allow students to create their own stages

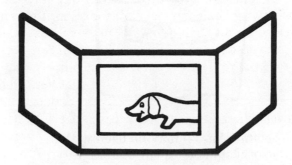

3-sectioned cardboard stages—fold flat for storage and can be used on table tops, allowing the puppeteers to sit in chairs

table or rocking boat on its side

upright table with a curtain

chair—makes a good stage for a one-person show

two chairs, a broom handle, and an old sheet—this works especially well with stick puppets

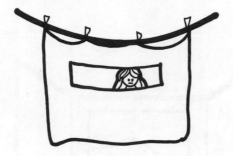

clotheslines—may be used with clothespins for a cut-out stage

clotheslines and sheets— this is convenient outdoors

discarded T.V. cabinet— makes an excellent stage

commercial stages—may be used with hand puppets or turned upside down for use with marionettes

SELECTED RESOURCES

A Selected Bibliography of Children's Books for Story Telling and Dramatization

Adams, Pam, illus. *There Was an Old Lady Who Swallowed a Fly.* Wilts, England: Child's Play International, Ltd., 1973.

Anglund, Joan Walsh. *Cowboy and His Friend.* New York: Harcourt, Brace, Jovanovich, 1961.

Bell, Gail W. *In the Strange, Strange Wood.* Provo, Utah: Brigham Young University Publications, 1972.

Blaine, Marge. *The Terrible Thing That Happened at Our House.* New York: Parents' Magazine Press, 1975.

Bonne, Rose. *I Know an Old Lady.* New York: Scholastic Book Services, 1961.

Bridwell, Norman. *Clifford's Halloween.* New York: Scholastic Book Services, 1966.

Brown, Margaret Wise. *Little Fur Family.* New York: Harper & Row, 1946.

Bruna, Dick. *The Christmas Book.* London: Methuen Children's Books, 1976.

Carle, Eric. *Let's Paint a Rainbow.* New York: Putnam Publishing Group, 1982.

Carle, Eric. *The Very Hungry Caterpillar.* Cleveland, Ohio: Collins World Publishing Company, Inc., 1979.

Freeman, Don. *A Pocket for Corduroy.* New York: Viking Press, 1978.

Freeman, Don. *Beady Bear.* New York: Viking Press, 1954.

Freeman, Don. *Corduroy.* New York: Viking Press, 1968.

Gag, Wanda. *Millions of Cats.* New York: Coward-McCann, Inc., 1928.

Hoban, Russell. *A Baby Sister for Frances.* New York: Harper & Row, 1964.

Hoban, Russell. *Bedtime for Frances.* New York: Harper & Row, 1960.

Hoban, Russell. *The Little Brute Family.* New York: MacMillan Co., 1966.

Holl, Adelaide. *The Rain Puddle.* New York: Lothrop, Lee and Shepard Co., Inc., 1965.

Holl, Adelaide. *The Runaway Giant.* New York: Lothrop, Lee and Shepard Co., Inc., 1967.

Isenberg, Barbara and Wolf, Susan. *Albert the Running Bear.* New York: Clarion Books, 1982.

Jewell, Nancy. *The Snuggle Bunny.* New York: Harper & Row, 1971.

Johnson, Crockett. *Harold and the Purple Crayon.* New York: Harper & Row, 1955.

Keats, Ezra Jack. *The Snowy Day.* New York: Macmillan Co., 1976.

Kraus, Robert. *Leo the Late Bloomer.* New York: Windmill Books, Inc., 1971.

Kraus, Robert. *Whose Mouse Are You?* New York: Collier Books, 1970.

Kraus, Robert. *The Carrot Seed.* New York: Harper & Row, 1945.

Leaf, Munro. *The Story of Ferdinand.* New York: Viking Press, 1964.

Lionni, Leo. *Frederick.* New York: Pantheon Books, 1967.

Lionni, Leo. *Swimmy.* New York: Pantheon Books, 1963.

Mack, Stan. *Ten Bears in My Bed.* New York: Pantheon Books, 1974.

Mayer, Mercer. *There's a Nightmare in My Closet.* New York: The Dial Press, 1968.

McGovern, Ann. *Too Much Noise.* New York: Scholastic Book Services, 1967.

McCloskey, Robert. *Make Way for Ducklings.* New York: Viking Press, 1941.

McCloskey, Robert. *Time of Wonder.* New York: Viking Press, 1957.

Minarik, Else Holmelund. *Little Bear.* New York: Harper & Row, 1957.

Piper, Watty. *The Little Engine That Could.* New York: Platt and Munk, 1954.

Potter, Beatrix. *Peter Rabbit.* New York: Frederick Warne and Co., Inc., 1902.

Rojankovsky, Feodor, illus. *The Tall Book of Nursery Tales.* New York: Harper & Row, 1944.

Scarry, Richard, illus. *I Am a Bunny.* New York: Golden Press, 1963.

Sendak, Maurice. *Seven Little Monsters.* New York: Harper & Row, 1977.

Sendak, Maurice. *The Nutshell Library (One Was Johnny, Pierre, Alligators All Around, Chicken Soup With Rice).* New York: Harper & Row, 1962.

Sendak, Maurice. *Where the Wild Things Are.* New York: Harper & Row, 1963.

Shaw, Charles W. *It Looked Like Spilt Milk.* New York: Harper & Row, 1947.

Silverstein, Shel. *A Giraffe and a Half.* New York: Harper & Row, 1964.

Silverstein, Shel. *The Giving Tree.* New York: Harper & Row, 1964.

Slobodkina, Esphyr. *Caps for Sale.* Reading, Massachusetts: Addison-Wesley Publishing Co., 1940.

Tazewell, George. *The Littlest Snowman.* New York: Grosset and Dunlap, 1975.

Teddy Bear's Picnic. Cambridge, England: Dinosaur Publications, 1981.

The Little Red Hen. New York: Golden Press, 1970.

The Three Bears. New York: Golden Press, 1965.

Tresselt, Alvin. *The Mitten.* New York: Lothrop, Lee and Shepard Co., Inc., 1964.

Viorst, Judith. *The Tenth Good Thing About Barney.* New York: Atheneum, 1971.

Waber, Bernard. *"You Look Ridiculous," Said the Rhinoceros to the Hippopotamus.* Boston: Houghton Mifflin, 1962.

Williams, Margery. *The Velveteen Rabbit.* New York: Holt, Rinehart and Winston, 1983.

Winnie-the-Pooh All Year Long. New York: Golden Press, 1981.

Zion, Gene. *Harry, the Dirty Dog.* New York: Harper & Row, 1956.

Zolotow, Charlotte. *Mr. Rabbit and the Lovely Present.* New York: Harper & Row, 1962.

Zolotow, Charlotte. *William's Doll.* New York: Harper & Row, 1972.

A Selected Bibliography of Story Telling Books for Teachers

Anderson, Paul S. *Story Telling With the Flannel Board, Bk. 1.* Minneapolis, Minnesota: T. S. Denison and Co., Inc., 1963.

Anderson, Paul S. *Story Telling With the Flannel Board, Bk. 2.* Minneapolis, Minnesota: T. S. Denison and Co., Inc., 1970.

Currell, David. *The Complete Book of Puppetry.* Boston: Publisher Plays, Inc., 1974.

Curry, Georgene. *Fun With Puppets.* Colorado Springs, Colorado: Current, Inc., 1982.

Engler, Larry and Fijan, Carol. *Making Puppets Come Alive.* New York: Taplinger Publishing Co., Inc., 1973.

Hutchings, Margaret. *Teddy Bears and How to Make Them.* New York: Dover Publications, Inc., 1964.

Hunt, Tamara and Renfro, Nancy. *Puppetry in Early Childhood Education.* Austin, Texas: Nancy Renfro Studios, 1982.

Jenkins, Peggy Davison. *The Magic of Puppetry: A Guide for Those Working With Young Children.* Englewood Cliffs, New Jersey: Prentice-Hall, Inc., 1980.

Karay, Haane. *Let's Learn With Finger Plays.* Bowling Green, Kentucky: Kinder Kollege, Inc., 1982.

Marshall, Kerry. *Pom Pom Storybook: Finger Puppet Gloves.* Salt Lake City, Utah: Zim's, Inc., 1978.

Osborne, Richard, ed. *Things to Make for Children.* Menlo Park, California: Lane Books, 1973.

Plush-Pelt Puppets. Omaha, Nebraska: Harold Mangleson and Sons, Inc., 1976.

Ring a Ring O' Roses: Stories, Games, and Finger Plays for Pre-School Children. Flint Public Library, The Flint Board of Education, 1977.

Tichenor, Tom. *Tom Tichenor's Puppets.* Nashville, Tennessee: Abingdon Press, 1971.

Vonk, Idalee. *Story Telling With the Flannel Board, Bk. 3.* Minneapolis, Minnesota: T. S. Denison and Co., Inc., 1983.

Wilt, Joy, Hurn, Gwen and Hurn, John. *Puppets With Pizazz.* Waco, Texas: Creative Resources, 1977.

Wilt, Joy, Hurn, Gwen and Hurn, John. *More Puppets With Pizazz.* Waco, Texas: Creative Resources, 1977.

Wilt, Joy, Hurn, Gwen and Hurn, John. *Puppet Stages and Props With Pizazz.* Waco, Texas: Creative Resources, 1982.